"Why doesn...

"Your father..."

"Yes?" Sammi reg___ ___ ___ ___ with wide eyes.

Caroline realized she shouldn't be telling Sammi what she thought about her father. She should be telling *him*. Ever since running into him in town, she had been hiding out, fretting over what he'd said, licking her wounds. And wasn't that symbolic of what she'd been doing her entire life?

This summer was supposed to be about confronting her problems and fears. And she was going to start with Reid McClure. Show him she wasn't the same scared young woman he had known seventeen years ago.

Dear Reader,

Welcome to Silhouette Special Edition...welcome to romance.

The hot month of July starts off with a sizzling event! Debbie Macomber's fiftieth book, *Baby Blessed*, is our THAT SPECIAL WOMAN! for July. This emotional, heartwarming book in which the promise of a new life reunites a husband and wife is not to be missed!

Christine Rimmer's series THE JONES GANG continues in *Sweetbriar Summit* with sexy Patrick Jones, the second of the rapscallion Jones brothers you'll meet. You'll want to be around when the Jones boys bring their own special brand of trouble to town!

Also this month, look for books by some of your favorite authors: Celeste Hamilton presents us with an emotional tale in *Which Way Is Home?* and Susan Mallery has a *Cowboy Daddy* waiting to find a family. July also offers *Unpredictable* by Patt Bucheister, and *Homeward Bound* by Sierra Rydell, her follow-up to *On Middle Ground*. A veritable light show of July fireworks!

I hope you enjoy this book, and all of the stories to come!

Sincerely,

Tara Gavin
Senior Editor

Please address questions and book requests to:
Silhouette Reader Service
U.S.: 3010 Walden Ave., P.O. Box 1325, Buffalo, NY 14269
Canadian: P.O. Box 609, Fort Erie, Ont. L2A 5X3

CELESTE HAMILTON
WHICH WAY IS HOME?

Published by Silhouette Books
America's Publisher of Contemporary Romance

For George and Jennifer Blankenship,
sister and brother-in-law extraordinaire,
in whose home this book took flight.

Thanks for the use of the pool, guys.

 SILHOUETTE BOOKS

ISBN 0-373-09897-9

WHICH WAY IS HOME?

Copyright © 1994 by Jan Hamilton Powell

Books by Celeste Hamilton

Silhouette Special Edition

Torn Asunder #418
Silent Partner #447
A Fine Spring Rain #503
Face Value #532
No Place To Hide #620
Don't Look Back #690
Baby, It's You #708
Single Father #738
Father Figure #779
Child of Dreams #827
Sally Jane Got Married #865
Which Way Is Home? #897

Silhouette Desire

*The Diamond's Sparkle #537
*Ruby Fire #549
*The Hidden Pearl #561

*Aunt Eugenia's Treasures trilogy

CELESTE HAMILTON

has been writing since she was ten years old, with the encouragement of parents who told her she could do anything she set out to do and teachers who helped her refine her talents.

The broadcast media captured her interest in high school, and she graduated from the University of Tennessee with a B.S. in communications. From there, she began writing and producing commercials at a Chattanooga, Tennessee, radio station.

Celeste began writing romances in 1985 and now works at her craft full-time. Married to a policeman, she likes nothing better than spending time at home with him and their two much-loved cats, although she and her husband also enjoy traveling when their busy schedules permit. Wherever they go, however, "It's always nice to come home to East Tennessee—one of the most beautiful corners of the world."

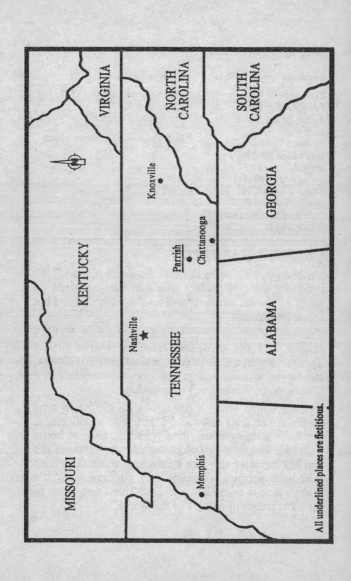

All underlined places are fictitious.

Chapter One

She remembered the tree.

Caroline gazed up at the massive oak guarding the entrance to Applewood Farm and whispered a prayer of thanks. Half her lifetime had passed since she had stood in this spot. For seventeen years she had done everything in her power to forget this farm. But thankfully, now that she wanted to remember, some memories were waiting for her. Waiting, just like this tree.

Filled with unexpected joy, she got out of her car, leaving the door open as she moved toward the tree. Branches spread wide above the crumbled remains of a gray stone wall. Leaves tossed in the breeze, green against the blue June sky. Both sentry and symbol, the tree was ancient, its roots sunk deep in the Tennessee

soil, as deeply entrenched in this valley as the roots of
the Parrish family.

"My family," Caroline murmured, and was startled
by her choice of words, by a rush of emotion. In the
years since she had run away, she had tried not to think
of these people at all, but when she did, it was always
as *the* Parrish family, never *her* family. Distancing
herself from those she loved and those she hated was
the only way she had survived. But that self-protective
urge changed with one step onto this land and this remembered valley.

She shivered despite the summer heat, her memories bringing a familiar, pounding fear.

But the same determination that had brought her
back to Applewood helped her battle the encroaching
sense of terror. She scrambled over the pile of stones to
reach the oak, and with a sureness born of instinct,
found a jagged scar carved into one side of the sturdy
trunk. Time had repaired only a portion of the damage. It was clear to see how a car might have plowed
through the brittle old wall and cut this gash into the
bark. It was so clear that Caroline could remember . . .

Nothing.

She remembered nothing.

Even with her fingers tracing the groove her mother's old convertible had left in the wood, she couldn't
recall the night of the accident or the three days that
followed. Those days were still a black hole in the
middle of her life. And trying to remember now filled
her with the terror she had fought so hard to defeat.

Caroline took a deep breath, disappointment gradually replacing the fear. She had known it wouldn't be

easy to open this locked corner of her brain. Just because she was no longer hiding from these memories was no reason to think they could be summoned so easily. Just because she had decided to come home . . .

Home. The word brought a shaky laugh. She gazed across the gently sloping fields, past the apple orchard from which the farm had taken its name, up to the square, red brick house that sat on an elevation similar to where she stood. Funny that she should think of that house, her grandfather's house, as home.

Caroline Parrish Tinsley's home was a small, pink stucco house in Carmel, California. Her home had nothing to do with an embittered, angry grandfather named Robert Parrish. Her home was not Applewood Farm.

And yet it was.

Surrounding her was the pungent odor of rich, loamy soil. From far away came the lowing of cattle, the drone of a tractor's engine. On the air was a rhythm, a pulse that beat in time with her own. This land called to her. And her heart responded.

But an unease remained. Aloud, she murmured, "You're not really home until you can walk into Grandfather's house." Could she really conquer the fear that had driven her away from here? There was only one way to find out—by facing that house and the memories she had buried.

Resolutely, she returned to her car. But before she put it in gear, she paused to pluck a framed photograph from her purse in the seat beside her. Two small children smiled up at her from the black-and-white snapshot. Because it was the only picture Caroline had

of herself and her twin brother, Adam, she had long
ago memorized every detail—the matching black of
their straight, thick hair, the way their hands were
clasped, the crack in the steps on which they stood.

She glanced toward the house, wondering if that
crack, where lizards had hidden in the summer, was still
there. Then she looked again at her brother's face. His
bright smile had always brought her courage. Today
she also felt a crazy, illogical hope. Wouldn't it be
something if Adam was alive, waiting here for her?
Wouldn't that be—

The blare of a horn cut short her wishful thinking.
A dusty, light green pickup pulled off the blacktop
county two-lane and onto the gravel drive beside Caroline's
red sedan. Heart thumping at the possibility of
confronting someone from her past, Caroline rolled
down her window.

Over the idling of two engines, a woman called,
"Something I can do for you?"

The height of the truck threw the speaker's face in
shadow, so Caroline got out of her car to see inside.
The driver was a young woman. Snub-nosed and
freckled, she wore a faded blue work shirt and patched
jeans. A red-and-blue baseball cap was shoved atop red
hair that had been tamed into a thick braid that draped
over her shoulder. Her face might have been plain except for her eyes. They were emerald green and framed
by thick, sooty lashes. And Caroline immediately knew
those eyes, recognized the quick, gamine smile the
woman gave as she repeated, "You need something,
ma'am?"

Pulse thundering now, Caroline said, "Lainey? Lainey Bates?"

"Yeah, that's—" The redhead blinked, then stared hard at Caroline.

"Don't you know me, Lainey?"

Recognition came with a flash of those fabulous eyes. In a flurry of movement reminiscent of the little girl this woman had been when Caroline left the farm, Lainey was out of the truck, her arms flung wide in welcome, shouting Caroline's name in a voice that broke. Her hug was rib-crushing and heartfelt. Caught tight in that embrace, Caroline allowed herself to cry, something she hadn't done in a long, long time.

But finally, when they had hugged and laughed and babbled emotional nonsense for several minutes, Caroline drew back, shaking off her tears. When she had thought of coming home, she hadn't dreamed of being welcomed with open arms. But then, she hadn't dreamed Lainey might still be here.

When she said as much, surprise cleared the younger woman's tears. "But where else would I be?"

"There's a whole world out there."

"I came from that world, remember? This is my home." The sudden proud squaring of Lainey's jaw made her look exactly like the young cousin by marriage who had regarded Caroline with unabashed hero worship from the moment they'd first met.

Lainey had been four years old when she came to live at Applewood Farm with Caroline's great-uncle and aunt. Caroline was six years her senior. But more than years, a world of circumstance and position had separated them. Caroline had lived in the big brick house, while Lainey had grown up in a small, frame share-cropper's house. Caroline's grandfather had done everything he could to keep the two girls apart. Yet Lainey's admiration and affection for Caroline had never wavered. Even now, after all these years, warmth shone in her face.

Grinning, Lainey said, "This land has a way of holding you, Caroline. Uncle Coy always said you'd come home, that you'd never be able to stay away forever."

"Uncle Coy." As she spoke the name, Caroline could picture the big, raw-boned man who had moved with deceptive laziness from the hay field to the dairy barn to the garden, wherever work needed to be done. His shoulders had been stooped from a lifetime of hard labor, his face lined, his big hands gnarled but still gentle enough to pat little girls' heads or stroke new-born kittens' fur.

Fond memories tumbled one after another inside Caroline. Good memories. Happy times. She had almost forgotten they existed. "God, Lainey, but I want to see Uncle Coy. I tried not to miss him, or you, or anything that I loved about this place. There was so much I was trying to forget, so much—"

"Caroline," Lainey interrupted, her emerald eyes shadowed. "Uncle Coy's gone. He died two years ago this fall."

She went on, explaining how his heart had stopped, but Caroline barely listened. Coy Parrish shouldn't be dead. He was as permanent as this oak tree, as this valley. More so. For hadn't he lived with her grandfather's hatred? Hadn't he lived every day of his life knowing that his half brother considered him worth less than the dirt in these fields? Living with that sort of contempt should have earned Coy immortality.

"...He just didn't want to go on without Aunt Loretta."

Caroline made herself focus on what Lainey was saying. "You mean, Aunt Loretta's gone, too?" It didn't seem possible that bright, indomitable woman could be dead.

Lainey nodded sadly. "You've been away a long time, Caroline."

"I know." Caroline's throat constricted by the threat of more tears. Finally she brought herself under control and nodded toward the house. "So he's got it all at last."

Lainey looked blank. "He?"

"Grandfather."

Mouth forming a silent "Oh," Lainey stubbed at the graveled drive with the worn toe of her boot.

"Lainey?"

The redhead met her gaze again. "Your grandfather's dead."

The world around Caroline tilted and whirled. She must have swayed, for Lainey took her arm.

"Lordy, Caroline, you're white. We'd better get you out of this heat and up to the house."

But the landscape stopped spinning for Caroline. "I'm all right. I'm just...just shocked, I guess." Why, she couldn't imagine. Robert Parrish had been an old man when she'd left. There had been no reason to think he might have survived the seventeen years since. No reason, except that, like Coy, but for opposite reasons, Robert Parrish had seemed indestructible.

"But he's dead," Caroline said, as if to confirm the fact to herself.

"I figured you'd be glad."

Lainey's blunt statement was too close to the truth for Caroline to protest. She let out a breath. "You never did pull any punches, did you?"

"Aunt Loretta always said what was just *was*," Lainey drawled in the matter-of-fact way Caroline remembered. "And I didn't figure many people grieved when Robert Parrish died. Least of all you."

"I won't mourn him," Caroline admitted. "But I did want to see him again. At least once. To ask him some questions." She frowned, considering what secrets the old man might have taken to his grave.

"Questions?"

Caroline met Lainey's quizzical gaze. She had a lot to explain to her. But standing in the drive in the afternoon sun wasn't the place to do it. "Come on," she said. "Let's go up to the house and talk. We've got seventeen years of catching up to do."

Lainey agreed, but before they could start toward their vehicles, a black pickup came down the narrow country blacktop, slowing as it reached the entrance to Applewood. A man leaned out the open window. His face seemed familiar to Caroline. His deep voice even more so as he called, "You need help, Lainey?"

The redhead waved him off. "No problem here, Reid."

Reid McClure, Caroline thought. Kevin McClure's older brother. Owner of the neighboring farm. And thus, her grandfather's enemy. As the man's identity became clear, Caroline half raised a hand in greeting. They had not parted on good terms, but she held no grudge against Reid McClure.

He stared at her, his expression unreadable at this distance. Caroline got the impression of hair still dark and curly, of a deeply tanned arm still corded with a farmer's hard muscle. She felt the shock of his recognition across the space that separated them. But just as Lainey gestured toward Caroline, he took off, his truck fishtailing back onto the road in a spray of dust and gravel.

Lainey shaded her eyes with her hand and gazed after him. "Now that's strange."

Caroline shrugged. "Does he still farm the place down the road?"

"You bet."

"And what about Kevin?" So many times through the years she had thought about Kevin, her dear friend and her first sweetheart. A few times she had gone as far as to pick up the phone to call him. But something, perhaps the fear of dragging him into her problems, always held her back. She had decided seventeen years ago that Kevin McClure deserved better than her. She hoped he had escaped the farm he had hated, escaped his brother's iron-fisted rule. "You knew Kevin, didn't you?" she asked, glancing at Lainey. "What's he doing now?"

The other woman's pained expression said it all.

Caroline let her shoulders droop and squeezed her eyes shut, stunned by the number of losses she was being asked to absorb.

"Come on," Lainey murmured after a moment had passed. "Let's go home."

With stiff, jerky movements, Caroline got back into her car. She followed Lainey's pickup down the narrow, tree-lined drive and up to the front steps. There she sat, staring up at the two-storied house, at the white pillars that cast shadows on the old red brick. She had done the impossible.

She had come back to Applewood.

"Did you hear about Caroline Parrish?"

Even though Reid had been expecting to hear her name for days, he took it like a kick to the gut. He looked up from the rack of magazines, steeling himself to see her. But in Parrish, Tennessee's newest and most modern supermarket, he saw no one with the wide brown eyes and sleek black hair of the woman who had been standing at the entrance to Applewood Farm last Thursday afternoon. A woman from whom he had scurried like a fly from a spider's web.

"Caroline Parrish." The repetition of her name made him glance at the checkout clerk. Sue Ann Melton, a thirty-something brassy blonde, was talking about Caroline to the elderly woman checking out in front of him.

The customer, whom Reid identified as Marge Donnelly, high school librarian, said, "Robert Parrish's granddaughter?"

Sue Ann pushed a bag of frozen potatoes over the electronic scanner. "I guess you remember that Caroline ran away."

"Just after her mother died in that car accident, wasn't it?"

"Folks said it was a wonder Caroline didn't die, too." Sue Ann sounded almost disappointed. Reid guessed the death of both mother and daughter would have added to the scandal of Linda Parrish's drunken crash.

Marge nodded. "Everybody was so shocked when Caroline ran off like that. Her grandfather tore half the countryside apart looking for her."

"I never would have figured her to do something so flighty," Sue Ann agreed. "We were in the same class at school. She was always so quiet. Maybe a little dreamy and odd—"

"Like her mother."

Reid's lips pursed in grim agreement with Marge's assessment.

Beeps sounded a staccato beat as Sue Ann pushed cans of soup and pork and beans along the conveyor belt to the bag boy at the end. "I always thought the Parrish money and name made Caroline think she was a little better than the rest of us."

Marge sniffed. "The money was gone by the time Caroline came along."

"All of it?"

"Robert Parrish lost the family textile mill right after Caroline ran away. He almost lost the farm, too. And for that matter, Caroline's real name wasn't even Parrish. Her mother ran off and married some native American. His last name was Cutler."

Sue Ann's mouth gaped. This was clearly a tidbit she had missed when amassing her information about Caroline.

"He was a Cherokee, I believe." Marge pulled her checkbook from her white straw handbag. "I hear Robert Parrish about disowned Linda for that. Why, I don't know. I met Cutler a few times and he seemed awful nice. Linda could have done worse. She met him out in California when she was visiting a college friend, I think. The two of them moved back here with the children—"

"Children?"

"Caroline had a twin brother. But their father took him and left Linda when the twins were about three. I heard the boy and his father were killed soon after. Drowned or something like that. That's when Robert Parrish had Caroline's last name legally changed."

Sue Ann sighed as she pushed a button to ring up the final total. She looked positively glum. Reid supposed it was because Marge knew more than Sue Ann about Caroline.

Marge handed over her check. "Now, what were you going to tell me about Caroline?"

"Oh, I almost forgot," Sue Ann said, perking up again as the cash register processed the check and spit out a receipt. "Caroline's back after all these years. Living out at Applewood Farm with Lainey Bates."

Marge sniffed again. "And I wonder what Caroline thinks about *that* one inheriting the last piece of Parrish property left in the county?"

Though Reid had no use for the object of the two women's discussion, he had heard enough of their gossip for one day. Particularly since they seemed ready to bring Lainey Bates, a person he happened to like, into their rumor-mongering. He cleared his throat, and Sue Ann looked up with a quick apology that turned to a melting smile. Her glance, like a caress, slid down his worn blue work shirt and faded jeans, making him flinch. She liked men almost as much as she liked gossip, and she had been after Reid since before Tonya had left him. But he would sooner wade into a pigsty than tangle with Sue Ann.

"Oh, Reid, honey, I'm sorry you had to wait," she gushed, deserting Marge without a backward glance. "But when I get to talking, well, you know." Her simpering giggle was almost as unflattering as her purple eye shadow and bright pink lipstick.

Before Reid could formulate any kind of reply, an arm shot around his waist, depositing a large bag of potato chips in his cart. "Yes, Reid, honey," a feminine voice drawled. "You know how it is when ladies start gossiping."

He sent a warning glance down into his fifteen-year-old daughter's mischievous blue eyes. But Sammi ignored him, turning her smile instead in Sue Ann's direction. "Hello, Sue Ann. Who are you skewering today?"

The blond clerk scowled at the teenager, but addressed Reid in even tones. "My, but isn't your Samantha growing up. It seems like just yesterday that she was a sweet little girl."

Sammi started to reply, but Reid forestalled her. "Why don't you go wait in the truck for me?"

"In the heat, Dad?" Sammi rolled her eyes, a relatively new affectation that irritated Reid to no end. She stayed beside him while he checked out, trading glares with Sue Ann. Her parting shot was a mocking, "'Bye, honey."

Once they were rolling their loaded cart away from the checkout area, Reid chastised his daughter. "I wish you'd make an effort to be a little less rude."

Sammi flicked a curling lock of dark brown hair over her shoulder. "Why should I worry about her? She just wants to get in your pants." Heads swiveled in their direction. One of them belonged to the new principal at the high school.

"Sammi," Reid warned, flushing. These days his daughter seemed intent on testing the limits of his patience.

"I just hope you aren't dumb enough to give Sue Ann what she wants."

He jerked the cart to a halt just outside the automatic door and caught Sammi's elbow in his grasp. "I don't want to hear that kind of talk from you."

"Oh, Dad, don't be so...so provincial," Sammi retorted with another elaborate roll of her eyes.

"Provincial?"

"That means—"

"I know what it means," he growled. "And I hope you know what I mean when I tell you I've had enough of you smarting off."

"Oh, Dad—"

"I mean it, Sammi, not another—"

Reid didn't complete the warning. His attention was caught instead by the raven-haired woman who had stopped just outside the In door.

"Reid?" Caroline asked, hesitating just as the door swung open.

He acknowledged her before he could stop himself.

She stepped away from the entrance. Resigning himself to the inevitable, Reid pushed his cart next to the outside wall of the building, well away from the main flow of traffic moving in and out of the front doors.

"Well...Reid," Caroline repeated as they faced one another. "It's been a long, long time."

"And yet it seems like only yesterday." Reid felt the look his sarcastic tone drew from his daughter. But for once Sammi kept her mouth shut.

Caroline rocked backward, looking puzzled. Reid studied her, saying nothing.

The years had been kind to her. He wasn't sure why that angered him, but it did. Her hair was still thick, black and glossy. Her figure still trim. Her olive complexion as clear as when she was sixteen and had ensnared his brother in a web of foolish fantasies. She hadn't been a pretty girl. She wasn't a pretty woman. Her features were too defined for beauty—winged eyebrows, full mouth and high cheekbones. Striking rather than beautiful, her face bore the clear imprint of her father's Cherokee heritage. Reid knew it was a face he wouldn't have forgotten, even if he didn't have reason to hate her. But he did. Therefore, her face was indelibly imprinted on his mind.

She bit her lip, obviously disturbed by his unblinking regard. He was glad. She deserved to squirm a little.

Sammi broke the tension by introducing herself. "My Dad isn't usually so rude," she said, directing an impish grin at Reid.

Caroline's expression softened as she extended her hand. "I'm Caroline Tinsley."

"Caroline *Parrish* Tinsley," Reid elaborated for his daughter. His emphasis on the middle name drew a glance from Caroline again.

"One of *the* Parrishes?" Sammi asked. "As in our county and our town?"

"I hope you won't hold it against me," Caroline returned, smile flashing.

With his daughter in tow, Reid supposed the best thing would be to move on. But he wanted Caroline to know just how he felt about her. He would have a lot of explaining to do to Sammi, but he couldn't resist saying to Caroline, "I hear you've moved in at the farm with Lainey."

"Not moved in, technically—"

"You mean, you didn't come back to claim part of the place out from under her?"

A line appeared between her eyebrows. "Of course not. The farm is Lainey's."

He hoped she could read the disbelief in his face. "Then why are you here?"

"I just wanted…" She hesitated. "I wanted to visit, that's all. I've decided to stay the summer, live out in Uncle Coy's old place, work—"

"Work?"

"I'm a writer—"

Sammi broke in again, suddenly excited. "Are you *that* Caroline Tinsley? You wrote *The Seers of Mycoglia* series?"

There was a brief, almost imperceptible hesitation. "Yes."

All vestige of poise deserted Sammi as she seized Caroline's hand and pumped it again. "Oh, my God, those are my favorite books. They're . . . you're . . . the best." On and on she gushed, naming places, people and events Reid supposed came from the science fiction and fantasy novels she read all the time.

It didn't surprise him that Caroline Parrish had grown up to write these modern fairy tales. Her feet had never been planted on the ground, and she had done her best to encourage the same silly notions in his brother. Those notions and this woman had been Kevin's downfall.

Now, watching his daughter's animated face, Reid was reminded sharply, painfully, of Kevin. Sammi resembled the uncle she had never known a great deal. In her coloring. In her slender build. Even more so in her temperament. Sammi, like Kevin, was a dreamer. Reid had no problem with dreams, but only if they were rooted in reality. He saw it as his job to keep Sammi anchored in the real world.

Now he stood quietly to the side, listening to the exchange between Sammi and Caroline, recalling the endless and, to his mind, pointless conversations Kevin used to have with her.

"I'm going to be a writer, too," he heard Sammi confess.

That didn't surprise Reid. At fifteen-almost-sixteen, Sammi changed her career ambitions almost daily. He wasn't going to get bent out of shape about that. But there was no way in hell he was going to stand by and let another person he was responsible for, another person he loved, be influenced by Caroline Parrish.

"Sammi," he said, breaking into the conversation. "You need to get these groceries to the truck."

"But Dad—"

"Now." He used a tone Sammi didn't usually cross.

With a long-suffering groan, she took hold of the grocery cart and said to Caroline, "Since we're neighbors, can I come over and have you autograph my *Seers* books? I have them all."

"Of course."

Catching his daughter's eye, Reid jerked his head toward the truck. "Get going."

He saw that Caroline's gaze followed Sammi all the way across the parking lot. Then she murmured, "She's like Kevin, isn't she?"

"Stay away from her."

Caroline looked at him, her brown eyes widening. "What?"

"Just stay away from my daughter."

"Reid, I don't—"

"I guess you know Kevin's dead?"

She closed her eyes, briefly, and Reid saw the muscles work in her throat. "Lainey told me he was in an accident. In Colorado, wasn't it?"

"Did she also tell you it was your fault?"

She made a choked sound. Her hand, slim and ringless, went to her mouth.

His anger at her over Kevin's senseless death, long-contained and compounded by time, threatened to overflow. It roughened, lowered his voice. "Kevin wouldn't have been out there if it weren't for you."

"Me?" Caroline croaked. "I don't know what you mean."

Heat rushed to Reid's face while his hands clenched into fists at his sides. "He was looking for you, damn it. The two of you had talked about going to Colorado, hadn't you?"

"It was just a daydream we had."

"Yes," he said with a sneer. "One of those daydreams of yours. After you disappeared and your grandfather couldn't find you and you didn't write or call—"

"I thought it was best—"

"Of course it was best, but Kevin couldn't see that. He thought he loved you. He went looking for you. And it killed him." Reid didn't trust himself to say anything more, so he turned on his heel.

But Caroline caught his arm. Her touch, soft and cool against his warm, bare skin, almost sizzled. He turned back, so that they faced each other.

"I never meant to hurt Kevin," she murmured in a low voice.

He stared into her eyes, hoping she could see the hatred he felt. He was close enough to catch the subtle, expensive scent of her perfume. Close enough to see the tiny lines that radiated from the corners of her eyes and mouth. Close enough to realize the passage of time hadn't left her completely unmarked.

She spoke again, her words slow and measured. "I never thought Kevin would come looking for me."

"Maybe not. But you can't change that he's dead. The past is one thing you can't change. But as for the future—stay away from me and from what's mine."

He slung off her hand and marched away.

Caroline watched his straight, broad shoulders until they disappeared inside his black truck. From the window, his daughter waved. But Caroline stood, rock still, too shocked to move as he sped out of the parking lot.

She glanced toward the grocery store, but her intention to stock up on supplies was suddenly unappealing. The thought of food left her slightly nauseous, as was the possibility of seeing more people from her past.

Until Reid McClure, everyone had been so nice. Just yesterday, she and Lainey had come downtown, visited the hardware store and the farmer's co-op, meeting and greeting people who had welcomed Caroline back with no questions asked. They had even stopped by the library, where the staff was so excited to have a native who was a published author that they had invited her to speak at a gathering planned for the first week of July. But now, with Reid so openly, surprisingly hostile, Caroline wondered what might lie behind other people's smiles. Lots of gossip, she imagined. As Robert Parrish's granddaughter and Linda Parrish's daughter, she had once been used to speculation. She didn't know if she cared for it now.

She drove home, taking the long route, detouring through the quiet streets of the farming community, down one country road and then another, pleased that her memory kept leading her down the right paths. Finally, when deep lavender shadows were stretching over the green ridges, she reached Applewood Valley and the farm where secrets were buried and memories waited to be resurrected.

The past is one thing you can't change.

Reid McClure's words made Caroline shiver as she drove past the farm's big house toward the small, white frame cottage where she was staying. Lainey waved to her from the doorway of one of the dairy barns, and Caroline was immediately warmed and reassured.

In the past week the two women had strengthened the bonds Robert Parrish had always tried to sever. It made Caroline feel good, knowing that Applewood belonged to Lainey now. When he died, Robert Parrish had left everything to his half brother Coy, who, in turn, had willed the farm to his wife's niece. Lainey might not have a drop of Parrish blood in her, but surely she loved this land as fiercely as any of the Parrishes ever could have.

Like the first Parrishes who settled this land, Lainey had come from nothing. A father listed as "unknown" on her birth certificate. A mother who'd deposited her here with Aunt Loretta and disappeared. Uncle Coy had raised Lainey as his own daughter, instilling in her a respect for this place and a particular way of life. With Lainey in charge, Coy's spirit lived on. And that spirit was the best of what remained of the Parrish family.

The very first night Caroline had been here, Lainey had talked of sharing the farm with her. She said Uncle Coy had always expected Caroline to come home.

The farm had been through some rough years, but when there had been profits, part of the money had been placed in an account for the time when Caroline returned. Lainey wanted Caroline to take that money. Caroline refused, just as she refused to become part owner. She wanted to leave things as they were. She loved this valley, but she felt the right person was in charge of Applewood. She wanted Lainey to use the accumulated money to do something good for herself or to make improvements or additions to the house or farm.

Lainey had eventually bowed to Caroline's wishes, but she'd insisted that Caroline must always regard this as home. She planned to make that legal, to stipulate that Caroline had a home here for life. And though Caroline hadn't driven out from California with the intention of spending the entire summer here, Lainey had convinced her to stay indefinitely. She had been good about giving Caroline space and privacy, and had understood when Caroline asked to occupy Coy and Loretta's old house. Lainey knew about the lost memories Caroline was trying to retrieve. She had offered her help and support.

Tonight, more than ever, Caroline appreciated the other woman. Tonight, Caroline needed solitude. She needed to write.

For as long as she could remember, she had taken refuge in words. When her mother's vague indifference and her grandfather's bitterness had been more than she could bear, she had put together stories in her head, escaping into fantasies. In the tough times after she ran away, when surviving had taken most of her energy, her only joy had been creating fantastic worlds where fear and pain could be conquered by those who were good and pure of heart. Eventually she had shared those worlds with others through the series of books Sammi had mentioned.

Fifteen books had been published in six years. But only two years ago had Caroline felt secure enough in her writing career to give up her job as a secretary and devote herself full-time to creating the *Mycoglian* myths her fans now wanted.

The books had continuing characters, a prince and a princess, twins, who shared the gift of precognition. They were the *Seers,* whose battle to save their dying race led them to face strange foes in even stranger lands.

Caroline was well aware that her choice of characters was a blatant reflection of her own life. That had been deliberate. Her brother was lost to her, but he lived within her books. Together, the two of them triumphed.

But no matter what worlds she created, she couldn't escape the past, couldn't get beyond the memories that eluded her. In this world, Caroline was haunted by faceless fears. Those fears stalked her in insidious ways, interfering with her personal relationships, controlling her sexuality, eventually destroying her marriage. She had tried running from those fears, had tried confronting them with the help of experts. Nothing worked. No hypnosis or dream therapy had ever broken through to the memories she had blocked or the fears that could paralyze her. That was the reason she had come back to this valley. To build a life or a future, to even dream of a relationship with a man or having a family, she had come to realize she must face and understand the past.

A past she couldn't change.

Those words pounded in her brain as she faced her laptop computer's blank screen. The latest installment of her *Seers* series was due at her publisher's by the first of October. Here it was mid-June, and aside from the sketchy plot okayed by her editor, she had nothing concrete on paper. And tonight, no matter how hard she tried to make him a blue-eyed blonde, her male villain insisted on becoming dark, with a face remarkably like Reid McClure's.

Reid. Who blamed her for Kevin's death.

Damn it, that was so unfair. So ridiculous.

Finally, head aching, she took an aspirin and went to bed. And as she had for seventeen years, she dreamed of rain. Of a violent storm and a boat tossing on the churning sea. But tonight, for the first time, the dream had a different twist. In pursuit of the boat, there was a dragon. Breathing fire in the driving rain. Bellowing like the thunder.

Caroline awoke from the nightmare drenched in perspiration. In every corner of the moonlit room, she imagined dragons crouching. She wondered about the change in the dream. Maybe that was good. Maybe it meant that coming here, where her past was close, was working. Maybe now, tonight, she would remember. She lay in the dark, waiting. But no revelations came to her.

And finally, when her heart had assumed its normal rhythm, she got up and began to write.

Of dragons breathing fire in the rain.

Chapter Two

The creek that separated Applewood from the Mc-Clure farm was called The Little Sandy, although there was more mud than sand to be found in the creek bed. It was a meandering sort of stream, wide and shallow at some points, narrow and rocky at others. In the heat of August the flow had been known to disappear. Spring rains often flooded the banks and surrounding fields. And as might be expected, there was one spot simply made for swimming.

Out close to the ridge, well beyond sight of either farmhouse, the water widened and pooled in a rock-rimmed bowl fed by the creek as well as an underground spring. This combination kept the water clear and sparkling. Moss carpeted the bank while trees arched overhead. Snakes had been spotted sunning on some of the larger rocks. Carp darted through the current. And an occasional deer came down from the ridge to lap at the cold, sweet water. But other than those intruders, most days it was quiet and secluded.

Uncle Coy had told Caroline that he had courted Aunt Loretta here with Sunday picnics and moonlight swims. Caroline could remember spending long summer afternoons swimming with her mother. That was before Linda retreated into her own vague, bourbon-scented world. After that, Caroline had disobeyed her grandfather's instructions to "stay away from the little Bates bastard" and brought Lainey here to swim and dive and play. And it was at this spot, under the trees, that Kevin McClure and she had first let their friendship blossom into puppy love.

Yet it was Reid McClure that Caroline was thinking of as she treaded water in the center of the pool. Indeed, since seeing Reid five days ago, a portion of each waking hour had been devoted to mulling over his accusations about her part in Kevin's death.

Maybe she did feel some guilt. But not real responsibility. She'd had no reason to think Kevin would come chasing after her. They hadn't really been in love. They had been young and impetuous, eager for a first taste of passion. But they were friends first. Their romantic relationship had never progressed further than the tamest petting. Seeing Kevin at all was a risk, but Caroline knew she would never have chanced her grandfather's wrath and become sexually involved.

Beyond that, Caroline had always known how wrong she and Kevin were for each other. He had wanderlust in his soul, while she wanted a settled home. Their dreams would have eventually collided. Half the attraction they had felt for each other had been because McClures and Parrishes weren't supposed to fraternize.

In the years since she'd left, Caroline had always imagined that Kevin went on with his life. She was certain that when he left home, it was as much for himself as it was to search for her. His death, which Lainey had told her came while working for a logging operation in Colorado, had been a tragic accident. Reid's blaming her didn't make sense. If the only reason Kevin had left was to find her, then why had he waited a full year after she was gone? That, more than anything else, should prove how little responsibility she bore for his leaving.

But Reid believed otherwise. Reid McClure was still as pigheaded and sanctimonious as ever. His way had always been the only way. Maybe that came from inheriting the responsibility for the farm and for his younger brother at a young age. He had been in his late twenties when Caroline ran away. That put him in his mid-forties now, although he didn't look it. There were a few gray hairs at his temples, but he looked as hardbodied and fit as ever. Quite fit indeed, Caroline told herself, remembering the strong legs and taut backside she had watched as he'd walked away from her at the supermarket.

She frowned, somewhat uncomfortable thinking of Reid as an attractive man. As if she had ever felt comfortable with such thoughts of *any* man. But especially Reid....

Caroline jumped as something crashed through the underbrush on the McClure side of the bank. Not something, she quickly realized. Someone. Sammi and an unknown male teenager. The girl wore a scarlet bikini top and a pair of baggy black boxer shorts. The boy, tanned and blond, was in long, neon yellow trunks. The two of them were intent on one another and didn't see Caroline, and before she said anything, they embraced and shared a long, deep kiss.

Floating downstream and leaving them alone was the option Caroline most wanted to exercise. But Sammi spotted her the moment the kiss ended.

"Miss Tinsley," she said, hurriedly stepping out of the young man's arms. She looked surprised but not discomfited. A testament to her poise, Caroline thought. "I didn't...that is, we didn't—"

"Expect to see me?" Caroline smiled, then paddled from the deep center to the shallower water near them. When her feet touched bottom, she stood, water sluicing off her modest blue maillot. "I didn't expect to see you, either. I've been swimming down here every afternoon this week, and haven't seen more than a squirrel or two."

The young man had turned to face her. He was tall and well built, with long, lean muscles. He slipped an arm around Sammi, a defiant tilt to his chin as he regarded Caroline.

"It's all right," Sammi told him as she dropped her big canvas tote bag onto a broad rock at the water's edge. "This is the writer I told you about meeting. Miss Tinsley, this is Kirk Williams."

"Call me Caroline."

Kirk smiled, a dazzling, charming smile that made Caroline understand his attraction for Sammi. "Nice to meet you, ma'am."

While Caroline reflected that there was nothing that made a woman feel older than being called "ma'am," the teenagers held a quick, whispered conference. It ended with Kirk waving goodbye and going back up the half-obscured path.

"Don't leave on my account," Caroline called. "I was just going to head for home."

But the boy waved again, and Sammi sat down on the rock next to her bag. "It's okay. I wanted to talk to you, anyway. If you come down here every afternoon, is it all right if I bring those books for you to autograph?"

"You're welcome to bring them over to Applewood."

Sammi's gaze shifted away from hers, pink tinting her cheeks. "I would, but...my dad, he—" She broke off, embarrassed and obviously uncomfortable.

Caroline had tried to forget about Reid telling her to stay away from his daughter. No doubt he had given the same instructions to Sammi. God, but that stung. She wasn't used to being treated like a pariah. But she also wasn't going to encourage a young girl to disobey her father, even if he was being unreasonable.

Caroline scrambled across some smaller rocks to the one Sammi occupied, taking a seat beside her. "What makes you think it'll be easier to sneak those books past your father and down here rather than over to Applewood?"

Sammi flushed, but patted her bag. "I always bring this down here with me. And I always have a book, too." With a flourish, she produced one of Caroline's earlier titles. "I'm re-reading this one. Have you got a pen?"

Caroline smoothed a hand down her bathing suit. "Not on me..."

"I'll bring one tomorrow with some of the rest of your books. And maybe then you can tell me about the new book you're writing."

The new book was dark and troubling. Caroline wasn't ready to discuss it with anyone. Least of all a young woman who wasn't supposed to be talking with her anyway. "I don't think you should be sneaking anything past your father."

Sammi raked her thick, curly hair back in a disgusted motion. "What's with you two, anyway?"

Caroline hesitated a moment, wondering exactly what she should say. "What did he tell you?"

"That he didn't like you, and I should stay away from you."

"Just like that? No explanations?"

Sammi rolled her eyes. "My father gives orders, not explanations."

Without thinking, Caroline retorted, "That's just what Kevin used to say about him."

The teenager giggled. Caroline responded in kind. And suddenly there was an ease between them, that rare, instantaneous rapport that sometimes arises between two strangers. Only Sammi's not a stranger, Caroline thought as she studied her young companion. Could someone who had grown up in this valley, on this land, ever really be a stranger to her? Their roots were the same. Beyond that, Sammi was Kevin's niece, and sitting here with her on the bank of The Little Sandy didn't seem so very different than it had felt to sit here and talk with him. It was like going back in time.

Caroline leaned back, bracing herself on her arms as she grinned again at Sammi. "You look like your Uncle Kevin."

"That's what everyone says."

"It's your eyes, I think."

"My mother's eyes are blue, too."

"Not like yours and Kevin's. Not cornflower blue." Sammi's mother, Tonya, had been a young bride when Caroline knew her. Caroline honestly couldn't remember much about Tonya, except that she was one of the few people who regularly stood up to Reid.

Sammi drew her legs up, resting her chin on her knees, her expression wistful. "I wish I'd known Uncle Kevin."

"He was a great guy," Caroline assured her. "Gentle. Kind." She thought fondly of the energetic boy with the dreams as limitless as the sky. "Kevin was unbelievably brilliant. I think he could have done anything he wanted."

"He's the reason Dad dislikes you, isn't he? Because you and Kevin used to go out."

"Did your dad tell you that?"

Sammi shook her head. "I could tell by Kevin's high school yearbooks. You wrote him a mushy note at the end of sophomore year and signed your name with hearts."

"Oh, yeah," Caroline said, remembering with a brief, sad smile. "I guess I signed everything with hearts back then."

"But why didn't Dad like you?"

As she sought a way to explain, Caroline felt a fresh spurt of anger toward Reid McClure. She had no doubt that if she weren't a Parrish, he wouldn't carry such an illogical, ridiculous grudge. There had been no love lost between the Parrishes and McClures long before she was ever born, ever since one of Reid's ancestors had won a portion of Applewood's original acreage in a wager with her great-great-grandfather. And now Reid sought to extend the animosity into Sammi's generation.

Caroline didn't give a damn what he thought of her. And if he didn't want Sammi talking to her—that was fine, too. The least he could do, however, was give Sammi his real reasons for feeling as he did. The girl wasn't a child. Lainey had told Caroline that Sammi would be sixteen this summer. But it wasn't surprising that Reid would treat her like she was six. He had been the same with his brother. When he issued an order, he had expected to be obeyed with no questions asked. And if Kevin dared press for an explanation, all Reid would say was, "Just because I said so."

"Your father..." Caroline fumed, fury making her voice tight. "Your father..."

"Yes?" Sammi regarded her with wide eyes.

Caroline realized she shouldn't be telling Sammi what she thought about Reid. She should be telling him. Ever since running into him in town, she had been hiding out, fretting over what he had said, licking her wounds. And wasn't that symbolic of what she had been doing her entire life? This summer was supposed to be about confronting her problems and fears. And she was going to start with Reid McClure. She was going to show him she wasn't the same scared young girl he had known seventeen years ago.

"Is your father home?" she asked Sammi. "I'm going to talk to him."

"When I sneaked off to meet..." Sammi colored, then cleared her throat. "I mean, when I met Kirk down at the old logging road, Dad was working at the machine shed behind the main dairy barn. It's—"

"I remember," Caroline told her, smiling again. "The machine shed is one of the places Kevin and I used to sneak—" she coughed "—I mean, one of the places we used to meet."

Sammi grinned in response. Caroline supposed it was terribly wrong to imply an approval of Sammi sneaking off to meet a boy, but judging from the girl's obvious spunk, no encouragement was needed.

"You won't tell Dad about Kirk, will you?" Sammi asked.

"I don't see any reason why it should come up. Now, let's go."

While Sammi went back up the trail Kirk had taken, Caroline swam to the other side of the pool, toweled off, pulled on canvas shoes and a long, loose T-shirt. She tossed her beach towel over her shoulder and set off. A short walk downstream, the creek flattened out and she was able to cross, hopping from rock to rock, and joining Sammi on the other side.

Across the field she could see the McClure farm. A number of dairy barns and various other outbuildings were clustered around the house, which was two-storied and white, with a broad porch that wrapped from the front around one side. It was a structure typical of those found throughout the rural South, a tall rectangle in front with one-story wings and additions jutting out to the side and back. The original house had been built just after the Civil War, torn down, then rebuilt around the turn of the century, just about the time the house at Applewood was given its current impressive facade. Both houses had received their share of updating and modernization throughout the years.

There was no doubt that Applewood was larger, grander. But Caroline had always preferred this house. Not for any outward reason. But because, before Kevin's and Reid's parents passed away, they had filled this home with love. That emotion had survived them, flourishing even under Reid's autocratic rule. Caroline might not have always liked Reid's actions, but she had never once doubted that he loved Kevin or that Kevin loved him. Unlike the state of affairs among the members of her immediate family, there had been no question about the affection that existed in the McClure household.

While Sammi slipped in a side door, Caroline slowed her pace as she passed the house. Her gaze lingered on the potted plants that lined the screened back porch. Yellow pads cushioned the porch swing and the rocking chairs beside it. The place looked just the same as she remembered, well-cared-for, comfortable. Applewood had that feeling now, as well, since Lainey lived there. And yet Caroline still couldn't bear to sleep in her old bedroom, couldn't bear—

"You looking for something?"

She glanced up in time to keep from colliding with Reid at the corner of the garage behind the house. Shirtless, wearing jeans that rode low on his hips, he looked hot, tired and irritated. Perspiration glinted on his face and shoulders and in the dark hair that covered his chest and angled to a vee over his flat belly. Muscles rippling, he shrugged into the work shirt he had been clutching in one hand. The light blue chambray was dotted with damp patches and streaked with dirt. His hands and brawny forearms were filthy, but he shoved his fingers through his tousled, wet hair just the same, leaving a black smudge on his forehead.

Caroline didn't realize she was holding her breath until she looked into his narrowed dark eyes. She let it out, slowly. Had Reid been this powerfully, blatantly virile when she was younger, or had she been too naive to notice? And why was she noticing now? Rampant masculinity wasn't a trait that usually mesmerized her. But today she couldn't stop noticing, couldn't help but be aware of his body or of the fact that she was only half dressed. Her thin bathing suit and cover-up didn't seem near enough protection. And yet why in the world would she need protection from Reid?

He folded his arms across his chest and stood with feet planted apart, pelvis thrust slightly forward, glaring at her. "Well?"

She swallowed, attraction giving way to the fear that inevitably came when she was confronted by a strong, forceful male. That fear was the response she expected from herself. But fear was one emotion she was determined not to betray to this man. So she squared her shoulders and stared back at him. "I just ran into Sammi at the swimming hole."

His generous mouth flattened into a hard, white line.

"Don't worry," Caroline hastened to reassure him. "We only talked ten minutes or so. I haven't done anything to corrupt her." She paused. "Not yet, anyway." The last words were an afterthought, a challenge greeted by a furrowing of Reid's brow.

"What are you doing here?"

"I think we need to talk."

"I said all I intend to say to you the other day."

"Well, that's just great," she chided. "You hit me with the news that you hold me responsible for Kevin's death, and you don't give me an opportunity to respond. That's so open of you, Reid."

"I'm not interested in your responses. I don't have to be open with you."

She glared at him. "You're the same arrogant man you always were, aren't you? It makes me wonder how you ever got lucky enough to have a kid as great as Sammi seems to be."

"I want you to stay away from her. You damaged this family enough with what happened to Kevin."

Physical violence was alien to Caroline's nature, but right now all she wanted to do was smack him. Instead she gripped her beach towel—hard. And she fought to keep her voice level. "If you're going to accuse me of contributing to Kevin's death, the least you can do is listen to what I've got to say about it."

His laugh was short and devoid of humor. "There's nothing you can say. You filled Kevin's head full of nonsense—"

"I don't know how you can say that. Kevin was too strong a person to be so influenced by me."

"Oh, really? Then why is it that until he started going around with you, Kevin was a good kid, a straight-A student with plans to do something with his life?"

"He was bored with school—"

"Not before you."

"He was bored," she insisted. "And you didn't help."

Dark, angry red stained Reid's cheeks. "I would have done anything for my brother."

"Except let him be himself. Controlling him was always what you wanted most."

"That's not true." Reid stepped toward her, hands now clenched at his sides. "You didn't know Kevin."

"And you did?" she said with heavy sarcasm. "You're the one who didn't know anything about him. He had his own ideas about what he wanted to do with his life. But you never listened to him, to what he really thought or wanted."

"And I suppose you did?"

"Damn right, I did. I let him dream about traveling, getting out of here, off this land—"

"Those were your dreams."

She shook her head. "You're wrong. I loved this valley."

"But you ran away."

"I didn't have a choice."

He muttered an oath. "Of course you had a choice."

"Maybe I would have if you hadn't turned me away." Try as she might, Caroline couldn't keep her voice from shaking now. "You do remember sending me away, don't you? The night I left town?"

Until now, Reid had largely avoided thinking of the night seventeen years ago when Caroline and Kevin had come to him, asking for help.

"I remember," Caroline repeated. "Don't you?"

Of course he did. Reid couldn't stand here, looking at her, seeing how much of the girl remained in this woman, and not remember that terrible night.

It had been storming. One of those summer cloudbursts that was more thunder and lightning than rain. Kevin hadn't shown up for dinner, and Reid had been none too pleased when he finally appeared with Caroline in tow. The two teenagers had been soaked to the skin and shaking when they came into the kitchen. Tonya made them wrap in towels, but Caroline hadn't been able to stop trembling. She had sat, teeth chattering, pale and silent. Reid remembered the way Kevin had put his arm around her shoulders and said she was in trouble.

Thinking he meant Caroline was pregnant, Reid had reacted with quick, harsh anger. Though he had ordered Kevin to stop seeing Caroline months ago, he had suspected his brother was disobeying him. He just hadn't been able to prove it. But here was proof, he had thought, and he couldn't stop himself from delivering an I-told-you-so lecture despite Kevin's protests.

Kevin became furious at Reid's accusations. But he didn't fly off the handle the way he had when the brothers had clashed in the past. For the first time, he had faced Reid eye-to-eye, like a man, demanding that he listen. His controlled vehemence had shocked Reid into silence.

Caroline hadn't been pregnant. Her problem wasn't nearly that concrete. Her mother had died less than a month before in an automobile accident. The sheriff determined that Linda Parrish had been drinking and was killed instantly when she was thrown from the car. Caroline had been in the vehicle, as well, but had survived the crash. A head injury had left her unconscious for days, but the doctors had given her a clean bill of health and released her from the hospital.

But the girl thought she was losing her mind.

As Kevin had explained it, Caroline couldn't remember how she had gotten into her mother's car, couldn't remember anything of the night before the accident. Reid didn't find that unusual, given the nature of her injury. But Caroline was coming unglued, trying to remember. She said she had to remember. She couldn't sleep or eat. Anxiety and fear were interfering with the simplest of everyday tasks. She had asked Kevin to help her. And because he didn't know what to do, Kevin had brought her to Reid.

But Reid hadn't known what to do, either. His suggestion that she go to her grandfather was met with near hysteria. She said she had tried to talk with Robert Parrish, but since her mother had died, he was sterner and more remote than ever. He had spent the month since the accident going through the house, destroying her mother's clothes, photographs, papers—as if he could destroy any sign that she ever existed. He had told Caroline to forget her mother. He wouldn't discuss the accident. He forbade her to mention it again, under threat of punishment. When his half brother, her Uncle Coy, tried to talk with him about that night, he flew into a black rage. That's why Caroline was afraid to go to her uncle or his wife for help. Her grandfather controlled Applewood, controlled their livelihood, their very existence. If her uncle helped her, her grandfather would be furious. She would never do anything to cause trouble for Coy with Robert.

Talking about her grandfather, Caroline had disintegrated into frightening, near-hysterical tears. Reid had felt helpless. He didn't care for Robert Parrish, but the man was Caroline's legal guardian, a well-known businessman, civic leader, landowner. Caroline had given them no concrete reason to distrust the man. If Robert was acting a bit irrational, perhaps it was understandable given that he had just lost his daughter in a tragic accident. Reid felt his hands were tied.

Kevin was furious with him. It took an hour or more of reasoning, but Reid finally made his young brother see that they couldn't take Caroline in or interfere in what should be a family matter. Though Reid felt sorry for the girl, he wanted her away from his brother. Now it was clearer than ever that Caroline had far too many problems to be any good for Kevin.

Reid insisted that Kevin stay home while he took Caroline to Applewood. At first, she seemed resigned to returning home. But halfway there she became hysterical again and tried to climb out of Reid's truck.

"You said I was crazy," Caroline told him now, her voice steadier than it had been. "You said I was as unstable as my mother."

Reid unclenched his fists. "You acted crazy that night, Caroline. I probably said a lot of things by the time I got you home."

"I was scared half out of my mind."

"You were young. You had lost your mother suddenly and tragically. It was natural that you felt alone and frightened. I thought you belonged at home."

"The way I felt wasn't natural," she insisted, anger snapping in her voice once again. "It wasn't grief I was feeling. I was terrified."

"But of what? You never could tell me what you were frightened of."

"Of my grandfather!" Color draining from her face, Caroline put a hand to her mouth.

"But why?" Reid demanded. "Why were you so frightened of him? I know Robert Parrish was a hard man, and I know he didn't want to deal with what you were going through. He was going through a rough time himself. But what had he done that made you so terrified that you had to run away?"

Caroline closed her eyes, her long, silky lashes very dark against the pallor of her face. "I don't know," she managed to choke out.

"You don't know?" Reid repeated, torn between sympathy and irritation. He felt as if they were replaying the scene they'd had that night, when she had been unable to put a concrete name to her fears.

Obviously struggling for control, Caroline twisted the towel she held. "This is the first time I've been able to say out loud that it was Grandfather who frightened me. Before, it was always just this overwhelming, faceless fear. Not just of him..."

She swayed, towel falling to the ground, and Reid moved forward. But she backed away the moment his hand touched her arm. She turned, hand braced on the side of the garage for support. Every muscle in her slender body was tensed. Reid imagined she would spring away if he tried to touch her again. Yet that was just what he wanted to do.

Illogically, unbelievably, he wanted to pull her tight against him, smooth his hand down her sleek black hair and tell her everything would be fine, that she was safe. He had done that seventeen years ago, after she had jumped from his truck and he had chased her through the rain. He had held her, let her cry herself to the point of exhaustion. He had considered helping her, offering her sanctuary. But in the end he had ignored the impulse, hadn't trusted his instincts. Instead he had given her the platitudes without the help. He had delivered her to the big house at Applewood Farm. Back to Robert Parrish. Back to the man she had feared.

Now Reid stood at her side again, feeling helpless, an emotion he hated worse than any other. In a lifetime of responsibilities, he had always taken action when presented with a problem. His ex-wife would say he acted too quickly most of the time. But he couldn't stand indecision. In his book, it was better to do something, anything, even if it was wrong, than to stand by, waiting for the appropriate response to present itself.

"Caroline," he said now, touching her shoulder again.

She flinched away. But she faced him. She was shivering despite the heat of the June afternoon. "I shouldn't have come over here, angling for a fight. I'm not good at confrontations. I never was."

She looked as fragile, as breakable, as one of his mother's treasured china figurines. Once more, Reid fought the feeling that he should have her in his arms, where she would be safe. The animosity he bore her because of Kevin took a back seat to his protective nature. Reid had been raised to be a defender, a champion. He had gone against those teachings when he'd taken her back to her grandfather all those years ago. And clearly, the troubled girl who had run away from this valley had returned as a woman with some demons still left to conquer.

"Let me take you home," he said, offering her his hand.

She shook her head, the color returning to her cheeks as her shivers ended. Some of the temper with which she had greeted him earlier flared again in her eyes. "Don't worry, Reid. I'm not crazy, no matter what you think."

He flushed because she had read his mind.

"I wasn't crazy seventeen years ago, either."

Pretending an indifference he didn't really feel, he shrugged. "I'm not really interested in debating ancient history with you. You see things one way, I see them another."

"And of course your way is the right way, the only way."

Hands braced on his hips, he glared at her. "I thought you didn't want to fight."

She took a deep breath, looking stronger and more in control by the moment. "The only thing I want is for you to understand that I'm not responsible for what happened to Kevin.''

"Of course you don't feel responsible," he shot back. "If you'd felt any responsibility toward him—"

"I wanted him to forget me," Caroline cut in. "I realized that night after we came here that my problems were my own, that dragging Kevin into all of it was unfair."

Reid immediately defended the implied criticism of his brother. "He was just a kid."

"And so was I." Her gaze was steady on his own. "I was a frightened young girl."

"That I turned away," Reid completed for her.

She took half a step forward, hands spread. "No matter what I may have implied earlier, I don't blame you for taking me home that night, Reid. I know you were only doing what you thought was right."

And yet Reid had begun to blame himself. Hindsight was a dangerous activity, one he had avoided for years. Now it struck him like a blow. If he hadn't sent her away. If he had listened a little harder to Kevin. If, if, if...

The questions beat at him. He reacted with anger. It had always been his best defense. "Have you gotten everything off your chest?"

"I didn't intend—"

"I don't care about your intentions. I don't care about what you think about Kevin or anything else. I'd just as soon not run into you again, either. I told you to stay away from what's mine. So I'd appreciate it if you'd get off my property."

"Dad!"

They turned together. Sammi stood just a few feet away, regarding her father with a frown.

"This doesn't concern you," Reid told her.

Face red, hands on hips, Sammi returned, "This is my home, too. And I don't want Caroline to leave."

"When you start paying the bills, you can start making the rules."

Caroline made a soft sound of disgust. Reid glared at her again. "What's your problem?"

"No problem. Only that losing Kevin didn't teach you anything. You still haven't learned that you can't control the thoughts and feelings and actions of other people. The more you try, the harder people will resist you and go in the opposite direction."

The words struck home, but still Reid struggled to come up with a suitably cutting denial.

She wheeled away before he succeeded. "Don't fight him over me," she advised Sammi. "Save your battles for something or someone more important." Then she snatched her towel off the ground and stalked away, moving quickly toward the house and the field beyond. Reid watched her go with a mixture of relief and disappointment. He didn't like knowing that she'd had the final word.

Sammi was glaring at him. "Don't start," he warned her.

She ignored him. "I don't get you, Dad. I'm supposed to be nice and polite to people, but then you go off on someone as perfectly nice as Caroline."

"There is nothing perfect or nice about Caroline," Reid snarled, spitting out her name as if it were a bad piece of fruit.

"And why is that? What is it that she did to Uncle Kevin, anyway?"

"None of your business."

Sammi groaned. "Oh, great answer, Dad. That really helps me understand what's going on."

"All you need to understand is that I want you to stay away from her."

"And if I don't?"

"Sammi, just do what I say." He couldn't help wishing for the days when a swat on the behind could deter her from mischief.

"Maybe she's right," Sammi said smartly. "Maybe I don't want to be controlled by you, either."

And for the second time in the space of as many minutes, a female stormed away from Reid. Normally he didn't allow Sammi to get away with that sort of disrespect and insubordination. But he didn't want to fight with her over Caroline Parrish, not the same he had fought with Kevin.

Some of Caroline's jibes had hit their intended mark. He had sought to control his brother. But not out of selfishness, as she had implied. But because he cared. Because he'd wanted Kevin to use his quick mind to do something important, something worthwhile, something that would make him happy. He had always known Kevin's destiny lay somewhere other than this farm. Reid hadn't begrudged Kevin his dreams or his ambitions. He had only tried to inject a little common sense into the boy's reasoning. And he had known that the last thing Kevin needed was to entangle his life with someone as obviously troubled as Caroline Parrish. Even before the car accident, Reid had found her vague and dreamy, as seemingly out of touch with reality as her alcoholic mother. Even if she hadn't been a Parrish, Reid would have deemed her unsuitable for his brother.

Being a Parrish made her completely taboo.

But it was something more elemental, more sexual, that made her so appealing.

Perhaps he was beginning to understand the allure she had held for his brother.

With a muttered oath, Reid strode toward his house. He didn't want to think about the way Caroline's thin T-shirt had clung to her slim but rounded body. He refused to consider the full, saucy curve of her bottom lip. Or the way anger had crackled in her midnight eyes.

Conflicting impulses flared within Reid. He wanted to curse her, shun her. Yet he wondered what it would be like to taste her, touch her. He didn't understand those urges, didn't even want to consider how Caroline Parrish could be so attractive to him. But she was. When she had come around the corner of the garage, he had paused for a moment, admiring the long, tanned length of her legs, the graceful line of her jaw, the peculiar combination of fragility and strength that clung to her. He had forgotten for just a moment that he hated her.

But he had to hold on to that hate. He had to remember that Caroline was to blame for the loss of Kevin. All these years he had blamed her. If he stopped blaming her, then who would be left? He couldn't—wouldn't—consider the answer.

Reid put aside all thoughts of Caroline and Kevin as he crossed the back porch and went into the farmhouse's big, cheerful kitchen. His ex-wife had redone the kitchen just before she'd left. The yellow curtains at the west-facing windows were faded from ten years of afternoon sun, and the green ivy wallpaper was peeling in spots, but Reid still liked this room.

His daughter stood at a counter, her back to him, energetically mixing something in a glass bowl. She didn't turn around, and Reid sighed. All too often over the past year, they had been in conflict. Over school, clothes, boys. And Reid hated it.

There were only two completely right components in his life. One was this farm. The other was this strong-willed, impetuous child. The thought of losing her, as he had lost so many things in his life, was more than he could stand. He hated these sulky silences she employed after one of their arguments. So he guessed the first step was up to him today.

"Are you making dinner tonight, Cookie?" he asked, using her childhood nickname as he leaned against the counter beside her.

She flicked him a withering glance. A woman's look of disgust, Reid thought, reminded uncomfortably of her mother, reminded that his little girl was no longer a child.

"I could cook," he offered.

She rolled her eyes. "Oh, right, and we'd have something deep-fried, soaked in cholesterol and fat."

"I do kind of have a taste for fried chicken."

"We're having *grilled* chicken. *Baked* potatoes. And a salad with this *low fat* dressing." Sammi thrust a spoon toward him.

He took a taste and promptly made a face. "That's just yogurt, isn't it?"

"With herbs and spices. It's good for you."

"But—"

"Let's face it," Sammi said matter-of-factly. "You've got to start watching your diet. You're getting old."

"Old?"

"What are you? A good ten years older than Caroline?"

He frowned. "What's she got to do with anything?"

Sammi just smiled, her mood suddenly as light as it had been gloomy a moment before. "If you eat healthy for the rest of the week, maybe you can have some fried chicken and gravy for Sunday dinner."

Thoroughly puzzled but unwilling to pursue the matter, Reid went out to supervise the late afternoon milking. The company of heifers and his two hired farmhands was preferable to either of the women he had tangled with this afternoon. With cows, at least a man knew what to expect and how to react.

The kitchen at the big house at Applewood Farm was white. White cabinets. White floors. White, ruffled curtains tied back at the windows. Caroline was startled the first time she saw it. Not only was it far different from the dark, 1950's decor she remembered, the room was much more feminine than one might expect from someone as unapologetically tomboyish as Lainey, who said she had redecorated just last year.

Lainey was full of surprises, Caroline decided, watching the younger woman cut into a three-layer chocolate cake at the kitchen counter. She ran this farm with the help of only one full-time hand and a teenager who came by a couple of days a week. She milked, mowed, plowed, planted and picked. She delivered calves, drove tractors and rode horses. And if she ever decided to give it all up, Caroline was sure she could find work as a pastry chef.

Caroline couldn't help wondering what her grandfather, who had once dismissed Lainey as a fatherless daughter of a tramp, would think of the woman who now owned his precious Applewood Farm. She imagined he had rolled over in his grave more than once.

But she tried to put her grandfather out of her mind as she accepted the thick slab of cake Lainey handed her. "You're going to make me fat if you keep cooking like this, and I keep coming up here every night to partake of it."

Lainey sat in the chair opposite Caroline's with her own slice of cake. "As Aunt Loretta would say, 'You're skinny as mama cat with two kittens for every teat.'"

"She did have a way with words," Caroline said dryly.

"She'd have something equally colorful to say about how pale you look."

Caroline concentrated on her cake and avoiding Lainey's insightful emerald gaze.

"Did something happen while you were swimming today? Something you want to talk about?"

Something had happened, of course. She had been able to say, out loud, that it was her grandfather of whom she had been afraid all these years. Some people wouldn't find that so startling, given that he had been such a malevolent presence in her life. But the fear that had driven Caroline away from home and had festered throughout the years was centered on the night her mother died, on events that had been wiped from her mind. Only today while talking to Reid had she been able to say what she had never been able to admit to her ex-husband, to a minister or doctor or anyone who had tried to help her remember over the years—it was her grandfather of whom she was deathly, terribly afraid.

Her fear now had a face. But why him? What had he done?

"Caroline?"

She looked at Lainey, realizing she had zoned out. "I'm sorry. I'm just tired tonight," she murmured.

She wasn't ready to tell the other woman what she had discovered. Saying it aloud to Reid had been amazement enough for one day. It seemed he was a catalyst for many things in her life. Her book had taken off after she'd seen him last week. Today there was this startling, frightening memory of her grandfather. Yet it wasn't really a memory. Not yet. The fears simply had a focus now.

Lainey studied her for a moment, but didn't press her for any more details. Letting a person be was another one of the redhead's many talents. The two of them sat together in comfortable silence for a moment before she got up and brought a dusty, crinkled cardboard box from the pine sideboard to the table. "I found something for you. It was in an old trunk upstairs that I think belonged to your mother."

In the first few days she had been here, when she was trying to stay in the house with Lainey, Caroline had attempted to search for something of her mother's that her grandfather might have missed when he was purging the house of her belongings. Not only did she yearn for a memento of her mother, but she hoped the search might rouse some of the missing pieces buried in her subconscious. She had stopped looking after only a day, haunted by painful and unwanted memories.

Now she regarded the faded green box Lainey placed in front of her with trepidation. "What's in it?"

"Something of yours and your brother's, I think."

At the mention of Adam, Caroline took off the lid. Inside were baby booties, rattles, a tarnished silver spoon, rusted diaper pins and a photograph. In it, two people, her mother and a man, sat together, each holding a baby in their arms. Caroline could only assume the babies were herself and her brother, and the man was her father. She had never seen a picture of the man who had given her life. Until now, she hadn't known what he looked like.

Lainey leaned over to touch the photo. Her eyes were dreamy, sad. "Your father was terribly handsome, don't you think?"

As she looked down into the man's strong features, a shiver moved over Caroline. The feeling intensified as she studied her mother. Linda Parrish looked young and happy here. Not as she had the last time Caroline had seen her. *The last time?* Caroline frowned. When was the last time? She remembered something, some expression on her mother's face. Terror? She concentrated. Yes. It was terror she remembered. And rain. Quick as a flash, a memory teased Caroline's mind and then retreated.

Sudden, sharp fear swept like a feather down the back of her neck. Outside on the porch, her cousin's collection of wind chimes jangled. The sound was eerie, beautiful, and yet somehow cautioning.

"Must be about to storm," Lainey murmured, going to look out the window over the sink. Thunder rumbled in the distance.

Caroline again felt the same strange tickle at the back of her neck. She had a powerful impulse to turn around. And yet she was afraid, so terribly afraid of what she might see. The fear was more than a tickle now. It spread all the way through her.

A knock at the back door sounded loud as a gunshot. Caroline gasped, dropping the photograph and stumbling to her feet.

"Caroline?" Lainey said, staring at her. The knock sounded again, full of impatience. Lainey went to the door and threw it open.

Reid McClure stepped inside, ignoring Lainey's greeting. He had cleaned up since Caroline had seen him this afternoon, but he looked no less irritated and no less imposingly male as he strode across the kitchen to her side.

"Where is she?" he asked, barely leashed anger in his voice.

Caroline just stared at him, still caught by an elusive, half-formed memory.

He muttered an oath and dragged a hand through his hair. Genuine concern replaced the hostility in his tone. "Come on, Caroline, where the hell is Sammi?"

Chapter Three

Reid wasn't accustomed to feeling foolish. He was usually cool, in control, rational. But as Caroline pushed open the door of the old cottage where she was living, he felt even more ridiculous than he had felt in Lainey Bates's spotless kitchen. A few minutes ago it had seemed like such a good idea to follow Caroline down here to see if Sammi might be waiting for her. Now he wished he had gone home. Damnation, why had his daughter pulled this stunt?

Caroline switched on lamps as she moved through the front room. Her voice held a distinct edge. "As you can see, Mr. McClure, there are no teenage girls hiding here." Shoving her hands into the deep pockets of her full, light blue skirt, she paused at the doorway to what he assumed was a bedroom. "You can look in here or in the kitchen or in the back bedroom, if you want, but I can assure you that I'm harboring no fugitives."

He attempted an explanation. "Surely you can understand why I thought Sammi might be here."

"Oh, certainly," Caroline replied tartly. "It's reasonable to expect a high-spirited teenager to test the boundaries their parents set up for them every once in a while."

Heat crept up Reid's neck, irritation replacing his discomfiture. "A father doesn't feel very reasonable when he goes up to his daughter's room and finds that even though she said she had a headache and was going to bed early, she's gone."

A look of genuine concern flickered in Caroline's face. "Is this something she does very often?"

"No," Reid replied. "If it was, I might not be this upset. I waited until ten o'clock, figuring she'd show up. Then I decided she had come over here."

"Why?"

He laughed shortly. "Because I asked her not to and because she is definitely in to testing boundaries these days."

"But she isn't here."

"I can see that." Reid cast another look around the room. He took in the faded rug on the floor, the worn but comfortable-looking plaid sofa and the old black trunk that served as a coffee table. A quilt-draped easy chair stood beside the front window. Across the room, a makeshift desk had been created by a broad piece of wood placed over two painted sawhorses. The pool of light from the desk lamp revealed a small computer, a printer and an untidy stack of papers and books. The room smelled like flowers, the same subtle floral scent worn by the woman who lived here.

The realization that he had memorized the scent of Caroline's perfume disturbed Reid profoundly. Scowling, he started toward the door. "Since Sammi's not here, I guess I'd better go find her."

"Isn't there someone else she could be with?"

"I called her best friend. She hadn't seen Sammi since yesterday."

"Sammi certainly didn't cover her tracks very well."

Already pushing open the wooden screen door, Reid glanced back at Caroline. "What do you mean by that?"

"Just that if I were a teenager who wanted to sneak out to meet someone or the other, I would have definitely told my best friend to cover for me."

Reid studied her for a moment. "It sounds as if you have a lot of firsthand knowledge about the logistics of sneaking around behind your parents' backs."

With elaborate casualness, Caroline fingered the collar of her sleeveless white cotton blouse. "Let's just say I was once a high-spirited teenager myself."

He let the door swing shut behind him with a bang, stepping quickly toward her. "If I find out you've been encouraging Sammi—"

"Oh, for God's sake," Caroline protested, her offhand manner disappearing. "I barely know your daughter. And for that matter, it's been nearly two decades since I knew you. What possible reason would I have for coming back here and trying to cause some sort of trouble for you?"

His answer came without thought. "Because I turned you away all those years ago."

She regarded him for a long, silent moment. Her voice was quiet and even as she replied, "I told you this afternoon that I'm not holding a grudge over that. I hope you'll accept that as the truth."

Given his low opinion of her, it would have been easy not to believe her assurances. But there was a sincerity in her voice and in her gaze that he couldn't refute. "Okay," he told her gruffly, "I believe you."

Slight sarcasm marked her soft "Thanks for the concession."

He looked toward the door and the dark night that lay beyond. The storm that had been threatening for the past hour had brought rain. They had driven through the first splatters of it on the way down from the big house. He could hear the water rushing in the gutters and feel the moisture in the breeze that blew through the screen door and the open windows that faced the deep front porch. He could also tell that the worst of the sudden storm had passed. The rumbles of thunder and flashes of lightning were moving away. But Sammi was still out in the rain. Damnation, where had she gone?

He had to find her. "If you'll excuse me, I'm going to try and find my daughter now."

Caroline came around the corner of the sofa toward him. "I could help, you know. Lainey and I—"

"I'll find her."

"So you know where else to look?"

"She couldn't have gone far on foot and in this weather."

"Maybe she met someone who was driving, a friend or neighbor."

He frowned. "Most of her best friends are fifteen, same as her. They're not driving yet. As for neighbors, you're the closest."

She hesitated, then asked, "What about a boy-friend?"

There was something about the way Caroline didn't quite meet Reid's gaze that made him suspicious. "You know something about Sammi and a boy?"

Instead of answering, she asked, "Isn't there someone? She's a bright, pretty girl. Surely—"

"She can't date for another two months. Not until she's sixteen, at the end of August."

"And, of course, because those are your rules..." Caroline's implication was clear. Rules, even his, could be broken. And because Caroline was someone who had once known quite a bit about breaking his rules, Reid didn't ignore her suggestion.

"Hell," he muttered, impatiently thrusting a hand through his hair again. "The way Sammi's been the last few months, she probably is with some boy."

An old-fashioned clock chimed the eleven o'clock hour on the fireplace mantel. Caroline looked toward it and then back at Reid. "Tell me something. Do you still turn in most nights at about eleven-thirty?"

"Why?"

"Because that's when Kevin always used to make sure he was back in his room, so that if you decided to check on him on your way upstairs, you wouldn't find him gone. Maybe Sammi figured out the same trick. Maybe in thirty minutes or so, she'll be home, crawling up the trellis beside the back porch and across the roof into the upstairs bathroom.''

Frowning, Reid crossed his arms, disgusted by how easily he had been duped. "So that's how it's done. I always wondered."

"Didn't you go sneaking out when you were a kid?"

"Of course not."

"I should have known that, shouldn't I?" Caroline chuckled, a soft sound that made Reid realize he hadn't heard her laugh since she was a teenager. That was no surprise, given the explosive nature of their meetings since her return. The surprise was the way her laughter relaxed something deep inside him, made him a little less anxious to go chasing off in the rain after his wayward daughter. He thought it might do Sammi some good to come home and find him gone, but his sudden reluctance to leave Caroline startled him.

Caroline was still speaking, her tone teasing and light, her eyes soft with memories. "After you married Tonya, Kevin said sneaking out got a lot easier. He just went out *after* you went to bed. Which was always early." Her laughter died quickly as she put her hand to her mouth, looking flustered.

Reid didn't puzzle long over her embarrassment. Her remark made him think of the first days of his marriage, a time he hadn't thought of for ages. He remembered mornings when he hurried back to the house and took Tonya back to bed as soon as Kevin had left for school. Afternoons when she sought him out on some pretext or another, only to wind up making love in the barn or in a field dappled by warm sunshine. Nights when they turned in just after dinner. The fire between them had burned so hot and sputtered so quickly. When the passion died, they had nothing else to share. Not even their daughter could hold them together.

"It feels like forever since then," he murmured.

The sadness and pain in his expression surprised Caroline. She couldn't recall more than a glimpse of his softer side when she knew him years ago. Certainly that side had not been in evidence this past week. But being reminded of his ex-wife obviously touched him.

Intrigued, she perched on the arm of the sofa and chanced another question. "Where is Tonya?"

His expression hardened. "Atlanta. She's got a great job and a great new husband, and she's as far away from the farm as she ever wanted to be." His bitterness showed through the matter-of-fact words.

"Does Sammi see her?"

"Very little. Tonya wanted to start over when she left here. With no hindrances, no responsibilities. That suited me just fine."

Of course it would suit him. Reid was a man who had always accepted responsibilities gladly. Caroline had to wonder, however, whether his broad shoulders ever grew tired of burdens and problems.

"Now that Sammi's getting older, I'm sure it's even more difficult—"

"Sammi was five when Tonya left, and the two of us have always done just fine without her. It hasn't been difficult." There was a challenge in his tone, as if he dared her to suggest he might not have done right by his daughter.

Caroline hastened to explain. "I meant that even without children I know divorce isn't easy—"

"Because of your parents?"

"And because my own marriage didn't work out."

"You didn't say you had married."

"You didn't ask."

Of course he hadn't asked. He had done nothing since she'd come home except accuse and issue orders. Maybe that occurred to him now, because Caroline thought he looked somewhat shamefaced as he said, "I guess I knew you must have married. There's your name—"

"You're right. Tinsley isn't a name I made up for the cover of my books. It's my ex-husband's last name. After I left here, I didn't want to be Caroline Parrish, and I was happy to change my name when I got married."

"Who was the guy?"

"Harry was a waiter in the restaurant in San Francisco where I found a job."

"San Francisco," Reid repeated, lifting an eyebrow in surprise. "You mean you went all the way out there when you left here?"

"I wanted to disappear. That seemed like the other side of the world. The night after I left, when the bus I took made it to Nashville, I had to choose another destination. I remembered seeing a postcard of San Francisco. Of the Bay, I think. I thought it was pretty. So that's where I went."

"No rhyme nor reason for the choice."

"Just as far from here as I could go."

Pleating the cotton material of her skirt between her fingers, Caroline allowed herself to think briefly of those first, frightening months on her own. The worst part had been her fear that somehow she'd be found and forced to return to Applewood. No other problem—the lack of money, the hunt for a job and a place to live, the loneliness, the threatening attention of strangers—nothing had been nearly as formidable as the possibility of coming back where her fears were so very real.

Straightening her shoulders, Caroline looked up, catching an emotion strangely akin to tenderness in Reid's face. It was gone before she could react, leaving her to wonder if she had imagined it.

He cleared his throat. "This guy—Harry—when did you marry him?"

"Too soon. He was in college, studying to be an architect, working his way through with a couple of part-time jobs. He didn't have much of a family, either. In fact, he was as alone as I was. So we got married, and it was a...a mistake." The word seemed inadequate to describe the twelve years of disappointment and pain she and Harry had inflicted on one another. But she wouldn't elaborate on that, didn't imagine Reid would be interested.

But Reid was thoughtfully rubbing his chin. "I see a lot of marriages that are just mistakes. I see plenty of couples just holding on because they don't know what else to do."

"That's what Harry and I did. Staying married was a bigger mistake than getting married. Because at first, we really needed each other."

"At first you always do," Reid muttered, half to himself. "At first, there's nothing but this crazy, mad feeling that you have to be together, that you'll burn up if..." Voice trailing away, he shuffled his feet, his gaze sliding away from hers. "Well, you know what I mean."

Flushing just as she had when she had mentioned the early days of his marriage, Caroline nodded her agreement. She flushed because talking about sex had never come easy for her. And in truth, she didn't have a clue about what Reid meant. She had never burned for Harry. The closest she had come to passion was the awkward, innocent necking she had done with Kevin nearly twenty years ago.

Reid McClure wouldn't understand that. A man like him, so physical, one who lived his life so close to the elements—he wouldn't know what to make of a woman who couldn't warm to a man's touch, who didn't know how to give or receive sexual pleasure. There was an aura of sexuality about him that no one could ignore. Reid wouldn't know what to make of her. Unlike the shell of womanhood she hid from the world, he was completely, openly male.

She swallowed, unnerved once more by thinking of him on this level. But she couldn't stop herself. She kept thinking, wondering, looking at him. Quickly the room began to seem too small. Or maybe he was too big. His hands, so broad and long-fingered. His torso, sturdy as a tree trunk under his cotton work shirt. He stood as he had that afternoon, feet planted apart, hips cocked forward, so that it was impossible to ignore the bulge beneath the worn seam of his jeans' zipper.

Her color deepened as Caroline realized she was staring at that telltale bulge. Her gaze flew to Reid's face, but if he had noticed her embarrassing absorption, he didn't show it. He looked kind of dazed himself. His movements were downright awkward as he backed away.

"I should . . . go." Again he eased the screen door open behind him.

"It's late," Caroline agreed, getting up from the arm of the sofa and moving toward him again.

"Sammi might not be home. She might not even be out with some boy." Reid passed a hand over his face, like a man trying to rouse himself from sleep. "She might need me, might be in trouble."

"Oh, but Kirk seems . . ." Too late, Caroline tried to bite back the name.

"Kirk?" Reid repeated, his expression sharpening. "Do you mean Kirk Williams?"

Trying to cover her mistake, Caroline said, "I think Sammi said something about a boy named Kirk."

"What did she say?"

"Just that he was cute . . . or something. I—I guess I assumed . . ." Caroline knew she was stammering. She had never been much of a liar. "I think she said she had a crush on him," she finished lamely.

Reid didn't buy that. He crossed the short distance between them with one long stride. "What do you know about Sammi and Kirk Williams?"

"Nothing . . . not really—"

"Tell me." His hands closed around her upper arms. Not painfully. Just with firm pressure. "I want the truth, Caroline."

Panic churned in Caroline's chest. Not because she had betrayed Sammi's confidence, but because of Reid. Of the way he held her. The way his dark-eyed gaze fastened on hers with sudden forbidding, intense anger. She shrank away from him, but his grip tightened.

A muscle jumped beside his thinning lips. "Kirk Williams is two years older than Sammi. He's a lazy troublemaker. I'm not going to let her get mixed up with him. You should have told me about him."

"But I didn't—"

"You knew all along she was with him, didn't you?"

"No, I—"

"I should have known not to trust you. I should have known..."

She fought the choking, spiraling sensation inside her, fought to focus on what Reid was saying and doing. She tried once more to get free, but she couldn't. The horror inside her was a slow-acting poison, impeding her movements, her reactions. She was slipping, slipping away from what was happening and to some other place, a dark place. She tried to stop. But she couldn't. She couldn't stop the slide...

He loomed over her. Tall and furious. His hands rough against her skin...

A voice snapped through her skidding, traitorous mind. "Don't lie to me, Caroline. Tell me..."

Don't lie, Caroline. Don't you ever, ever lie to me...

Caroline tried to struggle free, tried to separate what was real, what was happening, from what she feared.

...From what she remembered.

"Caroline!" Reid repeated.

At least, she thought it was Reid. It didn't really matter who was holding her, hurting her, calling her name. All that mattered was her fear. This blinding, suffocating terror.

Like a weed whose roots she could never destroy, the fear wrapped around her, cut off her air, paralyzed her. It wasn't new, this fear. She knew it very well. She had done battle with this horror many, many times. And yet tonight it was different. She had felt the change earlier in Lainey's kitchen. It was as if someone or something was waiting, standing just outside the boundaries of her conscious reality, beckoning to her, telling her that she could remember, giving her permission to see, to hear, to know what had eluded her for so long. And as much as she wanted to know, as much as she wanted to fill in the missing spaces, Caroline resisted.

Because her memory was too terrible, too horrible, to face.

She began to fight. With all the strength in her body, she fought against the hands that held her, fought the force that beckoned her down into that dark, closed part of herself.

"Let me go!" she screamed. "Just let me go!"

Stunned by her reaction, Reid stepped back. He didn't think he had hurt her. He hadn't intended to hurt her. Angry as he was, he would never, ever physically harm her. He had never hurt a woman in his life. But Caroline was trembling, violently. She had shook this way earlier today after they'd argued, after she had named her grandfather as the person at the root of her fears. But this was worse. There was a blank look in her eyes. She looked right at him, but he knew she didn't see him. There was something wrong with that look, something terribly, awfully wrong with her.

He reacted by instinct, catching her hands. Unlike this afternoon, he didn't ignore the impulse that brought her bucking, struggling body close to his own. He just couldn't let her stand there, shaking, obviously terrified.

But it wasn't easy to hold her. She fought like a wildcat. The same way she had fought him seventeen years ago, when she had tried to run away from him on the way home to her grandfather. But now, just as then, he held on, wrapping her tight in his arms until she fought no more. Tremors shook through her. Great, heaving spasms. Like sobs, but without tears. She wasn't crying. Not on the outside, anyway. Seventeen years ago, she had cried. Dear God, how she had sobbed.

"Go ahead," he crooned against her hair, as he might have to a terrified child, as he had done that night so long ago. "It's okay if you cry it out, Caroline."

But she wasn't a child now; she didn't cry. And he wasn't the same as he had been back then, either. For tonight, his reaction to her was complicated by more than sympathy or irritation. The soft scent that swirled around him and the gentle curves that fit so easily against him were flagrant reminders that it was a woman he held. A woman he was supposed to hate.

He wasn't sure how long they stood that way, with him holding her, soothing her. He lost track of the time, lost awareness of everything but her trembling body, her breath that caught in little hitches of fading hysteria. She was so slim, so vulnerable. And he was the only barrier separating her from some yawning precipice.

She finally stopped shaking. This time when she stirred in his arms, he let her go. And when she looked at him, he knew she was really seeing him. Pale and shaken, she just stared at him for a moment.

"Oh, God," she murmured, her hand going to the pulse he could see beating at her throat. "Oh, God, Reid, I'm so sorry—"

"It's..." He faltered, feeling more awkward now that she was out of his arms than he had felt with her in them. "It's okay, Caroline."

"No, it's not okay." She sank down on the couch and leaned forward, covering her face with her hands. He let her sit that way for a few minutes.

"Listen..." he began, then cleared his throat. He stepped forward, hand outstretched, as if to stroke her hair, then jerked back, feeling as if he had brushed his fingers across an open flame.

She looked up at him, ebony eyes damp with the tears she hadn't shed before. "I guess you think I'm insane."

He phrased his answer carefully. "It's pretty clear that something's wrong."

She drew in a deep breath and let it out slowly. "There's been something wrong for a long, long time, since the night Mother died."

He was shocked. "It's the same thing that made you run away? After all these years, after your grandfather is dead, you're still afraid?"

She nodded. "I still can't remember what happened the night of the accident. I don't know why I was so frightened of him."

"And that's at the root of your—" he cast about for the proper word and made a sweeping gesture with his hands "—the root of this?"

"The proper word for it is a panic attack."

He shook his head. "This was more than panic. This was cra—" He caught himself before passing judgment as he had done years ago.

But Caroline clearly knew what he meant. "You think it's crazy, that I'm crazy. You always have. You made it clear that you thought I was just like my mother, and everyone knew how she was."

"Caroline, I . . ."

She held up a hand to stop his apology. "It's okay, Reid. Something, my grandfather most likely, drove my mother to the edge of insanity, and she was trying to drink herself the rest of the way. But it wasn't until the accident that this nightmare began for me. That's when the panic and the fear started. They've been with me ever since."

He sat down on the old trunk in front of the couch. "Maybe you need some help, Caroline."

She actually laughed. The sound broke through her threatening tears like the wind gusting down the valley on a humid day in mid-August. Unexpected and sudden, it caught Reid off guard.

"Don't worry," she advised him. "I'm not going hysterical on you again. It's just so like you to tell me— after seventeen years have gone by—that I should go get some help. As if I just sat around until now, waiting for someone like you to make the suggestion."

Stung, he leaned back, prepared to get to his feet. "All right, then—"

"God, Reid." Caroline put out her hand, scooting forward to the edge of the couch, so that her knees brushed his. "I wasn't trying to make you mad. It's just that I didn't spend the last seventeen years having one panic attack after another without trying to make them stop."

"And nothing helped?"

"Sure it did. Though you probably don't believe it after what just happened, I have learned how to control this a little better. Days, months have gone by when I don't even think about the reasons why I left here. But there are some things..." She paused, her gaze skipping away from his. "There are some things that have always triggered...reactions."

"Like someone growing angry. Or taking hold of you." Though unsure of his reasons for touching her, Reid leaned forward and placed his hands on her upper arms, just as he had before.

But she didn't flinch. Or try to shrug off his touch. She just looked at him, her eyes as dark and deep as the blackest part of the night. Common sense told him to back away, but Reid left his hands where they were.

"I guess the real trigger is the anger," he murmured.

She didn't answer. Her gaze simply remained on his, dark and yet somewhat surprised.

"I guess when someone comes at you like a raving maniac, like I did—"

"Reid, you didn't do that. You didn't hurt me."

"I wasn't trying to hurt or frighten you. I was just angry, and I took hold of you because I—"

"Was worried about Sammi."

Mention of his daughter made him pull away. He should be home, making sure Sammi was safe, instead of here with this troubled and troubling woman. He should be thinking about his responsibilities instead of the warm silkiness of Caroline's skin. He should run as hard and fast as possible away from Caroline Parrish.

He stood, but it was impossible for him to just walk out. Not just yet. "Are you going to be all right?" he asked.

"Of course."

He wasn't sure. She looked strained, worried, somehow haunted. "I could take you up to Lainey's."

She shivered. "I can't sleep in that house."

"You can't? Why?"

"I don't know." She got to her feet and rubbed her bare arms as if deeply chilled. "I just can't."

"Lainey could stay here—"

"No, I'll be fine here. I've been fine since I moved in here."

"But you don't seem fine."

"Listen, I came back here to try and figure out what it is I can't remember. It's something I have to do on my own. I can handle it."

"I still think—"

"Stop it." She cut him off with soft finality. "You're not responsible for this, Reid. You're not responsible for me."

She was a mind reader, he decided. Or a witch. Maybe both. For he felt as if he should stay, should do something more for her.

"I can take care of myself," she said.

He wasn't at all sure of that. Not after what had just transpired in this room.

"Go home to Sammi," she told him when he continued to hesitate.

He knew that was the most sensible thing he could do. After a final, searching look at her weary face, he turned. She followed him to the door and out onto the front porch.

The rain had stopped, and the moon was trying to put in an appearance. Glancing at Caroline, Reid saw that the light touched her striking features, shadows throwing them into sharp relief. She looked like a shadow herself—pale and slender, fragile enough to disappear if the light shifted ever so slightly.

Reid told himself he should just leave. Just walk down the steps, get in the car and drive home where he belonged. The worse thing he could do was stand here, studying the way Caroline Parrish looked in the moonlight. He made it to the first step before she said his name and he turned to face her again.

"I really didn't know Sammi was with Kirk."

For the second time that night he chose to believe her. "All right."

"I saw the two of them down by the creek, but she didn't tell me anything about sneaking out to meet him tonight."

"I wish you had told me when I came over here looking for her."

"I should have."

He was surprised. "You're agreeing with me?"

She pushed her hair back from her face and sighed, a long, tired sound that brought a reaction from somewhere deep inside Reid. "No matter what I think of your parenting methods, when you came over here so worried about her, I should have told you everything I knew. I'm really not trying to cause any trouble for you."

But she already had. She was trouble, through and through, always had been. But knowing that didn't do much to send Reid on his way. He still paused on the step, his eyes just about level with hers.

She put out her hand. "Thanks."

He enfolded her fingers in his own without thinking, the gesture bringing her that much closer. She didn't pull her hand away. "Why are you thanking me?"

"For being here, I guess."

"If I hadn't been here, you might not have had this panic attack."

Caroline shook her head. What had happened tonight had been building for days, fueled by the familiarity of her surroundings, by the memories that were trying to force their way back. "You were just the trigger, Reid. If it wasn't you, it would have been something or someone else. I came back here in order to remember. I need to remember." Though that was true, she shivered again. Maybe there really were some memories that deserved to stay buried.

"Hey, you all right?" He touched the side of her face with the hand that wasn't gripping hers.

Amazingly, Caroline didn't jerk away. No, pulling back didn't occur to her. What she considered was stepping forward, back into his strong arms, back where she could feel the solid strength of his muscles and smell the clean scent of earth and sky and rain that clung to his clothes and skin. If she moved just a fraction of a step, she knew he would enfold her in his embrace again. And God, how she wanted to be held. She could barely remember wanting to be held the way she wanted Reid McClure to hold her. It was ironic. He seemed to despise her, yet earlier he hadn't hesitated to hold her with such kindness, such warmth and gentleness. His touch had both comforted and stirred her. She had felt protected and wanted.

Yes, *wanted.* It was an amazing thought.

She could feel the attraction that was running between them, strong as a steel girder and as elusive as the moonbeams that were dancing around them. For her entire adult life she had sought to avoid this sort of sexual undercurrent. But not now. Not with Reid. Now she followed the pull.

The playful moonlight hid his expression from her, but if she stepped forward, if she...

"Caroline." Her name was a husky whisper, part entreaty, part warning, as he brushed his fingers from her cheek to her hair. Close as she was now, she could see his face, see his confusion and wariness, as he murmured, "Caroline Parrish."

Her name snapped the tension between them. Her name made him suck in his breath, pull away from her and go down the front steps to his waiting truck. And though she wanted to call him back, she let him go.

She stood on the front porch, watching his taillights as he drove around the cluster of dairy barns and out-buildings. His truck followed the driveway up to the big house, where it seemed to pause a moment before dis-appearing altogether. Soon even the sound of the en-gine was gone.

And Caroline was alone. Alone with the sounds of a summer night at Applewood, the last of the rain dripping from tree leaves, the frogs singing down at the creek. Alone with a dark, faceless memory that once again was hammering at the locked corner of her mind. Alone, without anyone's arms to hold her.

She went inside and, crazily, irrationally, bolted her door and the windows. The terror was inside, not out. The terror had her grandfather's face, and he was gone. But the locks seemed necessary. Even with that security, she still paced the room. Even the photo-graph of her and her brother Adam, the one that had always reassured her, failed to bring its usual sense of well-being and peace. Her pulse didn't slow until she curled up on the couch, closed her eyes and remem-bered being in Reid's arms.

And that night, the dragon didn't chase through her dreams.

"Dadblastit!" The exclamation was followed by a string of fouler, more colorful curses as Reid cut the engine on his tractor. From the amount of billowing steam, he imagined the radiator he had repaired just last week was on the fritz again. The hiss of escaping water vapor underscored his sinking feeling.

He climbed off the machine, tugged off his baseball cap and used the back of his arm to brush the sweat from his eyes. An accusatory glance at the cloudless sky was followed by another curse. Not quite ten in the morning and already the temperature was soaring and the humidity level was nearing a hundred percent. By this afternoon, after he got this tractor running again, mowing this field would be an even more sweltering task. *If* he could fix the tractor, that was. That was a substantial if.

The way his week had gone, he would probably need a new radiator instead of just a repair. Ever since he had almost kissed Caroline Parrish in the moonlight, his luck had been running from bad to worse. Sammi wasn't speaking to him. Milk production was down. Crows had descended on the cornfield. And his best farmhand was laid up with a torn ligament in his leg.

Though he had felt downright bewitched when he'd left her place that night, Reid didn't want to think Caroline had anything to do with his bum run of luck. He didn't want to think about her at all. But his mind was turning traitor these days, and she popped into his head at odd moments, interfering with his work, robbing him of sleep and generally disrupting his life.

"Which is exactly what I would expect from a Parrish."

Blowing out a disgusted breath instead of cursing again, Reid allowed himself to sag momentarily against the big wheel of the aging piece of machinery. He felt hot and tired and defeated. If he could afford it, he would drive into town this afternoon and come home with a brand new tractor, a big, heavy-duty job, with an enclosed, air-conditioned driver's seat. But even though the farm had experienced several good years in a row, he had recently purchased the strip of land he was mowing, and money was tight. Somehow, some way, he had to coax a few more years' worth of work out of this old clunker.

Unbidden, a picture of Caroline Parrish's expensive, red foreign sedan sprang to mind. He shrugged off the thought even as he fitted his cap back on his head. He was *not* going to waste his energy thinking about her.

Instead he patted the dinted and once-bright blue fender that covered the tractor wheel. "All right, you old harridan, let's see what you've done to me now."

The radiator was still gushing steam and hot water, but Reid tried to check it anyway, and in the process burned the back of the fingers on his left hand. The pain was quick and sharp and sent him leaping away from the tractor, clutching his hand and spewing curses at the machine again.

It was clear that his best bet was to let this sucker cool off before attempting any major investigation of the problem. He could walk back to the barn and drive his pickup back out with his tools. He spared another glance at the sky. "Tearing this apart out here in the heat ought to be a whole lot of fun." But with his luck, any attempt to drive it back to the machine shed would undoubtedly cause even more expensive damage. So he swung the insulated jug that held some water off the platform beside the seat and struck off across the fields toward home, his hand throbbing and a headache beginning just behind his eyes.

He was facing quite a walk. The field he had been mowing was at the edge of his property, some distance from the house and the barns. Reid had purchased this acreage from his neighbor on the opposite side of Applewood, but all three farms had once met at a point near here. The shortest route home was to follow the creek that separated his place from Applewood.

He gazed at his land with pleased satisfaction as he neared the creek. His father would be happy to see the way Reid had expanded their holdings. The real coup would have been snagging a piece of Applewood. Reid had been making offers since Robert Parrish had passed on, but first Coy and then Lainey had rejected even a premium price.

Reid grinned, thinking about Lainey's stubborn refusal to part with an inch of land. Several folks in the community had made some not-so-sly suggestions about his and Lainey getting together. From an economic standpoint, it made some sense, combining their two successful dairy farms into one big operation. But he couldn't imagine entertaining romantic thoughts about Lainey, a woman he had watched grow up.

Funny how that didn't keep him from having those thoughts about Caroline.

With a sigh, Reid stopped in a stand of cedars and pines near the creek. Lord, but he didn't know why he couldn't shake this fascination with Caroline. He hated her, didn't he? She was the reason Kevin had run away, wasn't she? And she was a Parrish. She might have distanced herself from this place, but that blood still ran in her veins. That meant he shouldn't trust her.

Pondering that, he took a long, deep gulp of the lukewarm water he had carried with him. It provided so little refreshment that he took off his cap and up-ended the bottle over his injured hand and then his head. Water streamed over his hair, wet his neck and chest, but even that didn't do much to dull the burn of his fingers, combat the heat or clear his muddied thinking.

Ever since he had run into Caroline, he had done nothing but think. Aside from the strange effect she had on his libido, some of the things she had said troubled him profoundly. For instance, she had said he was the one at fault with his brother, that he hadn't known him. She implied he might be more to blame for Kevin's fate than she was.

He didn't want to consider that any more than he wanted to think about the tender emotions she roused in him. *Tender?* The word made him laugh out loud. Even though he had offered her comfort, there had been nothing tender about the need and the want she had awakened in his gut. That emotion was purely, powerfully sexual. She had felt the attraction, as well. He had seen it in her face, felt it in the way she had swayed close to him. She had been just as tempted, just as turned on, as he.

"But I could probably be turned on by a stump," Reid told himself, trying to find an excuse for his feelings. He hadn't been on a date in months, not since the woman he had been halfheartedly courting had gotten tired of him. She'd said he was just using her for sex. Maybe he had been. Funny thing was, he thought she was getting some pleasure out of the relationship, too.

But no. She had wanted a commitment, and he wasn't interested.

So maybe it was understandable that holding Caroline had roused a sexual response. It had to do with basic biological urges, not with her in particular. Perhaps his response to her was particularly strong, but that didn't mean anything. What he should do was get out and meet some nice woman who wouldn't make any demands. He certainly didn't want to become entangled with a woman as needy and troubled as Caroline. He had his hands full trying to make a living and raising his daughter.

Sammi.

Reid sighed. Just thinking about his headstrong daughter made him wish for another jug of water to dump over his head.

She had been in her bed when he got home from Caroline's last week. She had looked so innocent, pretending to rub her eyes and yawn when he switched on the light in her room. She claimed to have been asleep for hours, but the wet clothes she had left on the floor gave her away. As did the muddy footprints leading from her bathroom window. Now she was grounded. Reid had assigned a couple of dozen chores to keep her busy during her enforced confinement.

He had heard her on the phone last night, telling her best friend that he was a dinosaur. Maybe he was. Maybe he was old-fashioned and as ferociously controlling as Caroline had said. But he would not relent and allow Sammi to see a boy he knew was trouble.

Kirk Williams's father, Doyle, owned and operated the town's most successful real estate firm. Doyle and his wife were divorced, but she was from a wealthy family, and their son had everything handed to him. He didn't work, like most boys his age, didn't even play a sport that Reid knew of. No, Reid had never seen Kirk do anything but cruise around in his expensive car.

Kirk had so much time on his hands, he and some of his buddies had vandalized the high school late last winter. "Just for kicks" was the only reason Reid had heard they gave. They were suspended from school for a month and their parents had to pay for the damages, but from what Reid saw of the crowd that hung out in the discount store's parking lot and at the hamburger spot in town, none of these spoiled boys had learned their lesson. And he'd be damned if any of them would get a chance to spoil his daughter.

He grew angry at the thought and started out from beneath the shade of the trees with renewed vigor. But he quickly shrank back in the shadows. For on the path that ran along the creek, he spied Sammi.

She wore her bathing suit top and shorts, a towel slung over her shoulder and a tote bag swinging at her side. Nothing strange about that since she appeared to be headed toward the swimming hole. But Reid had left her with plenty to do this morning. It was possible that she was finished with her chores, but it was also possible that she was up to no good.

Eyes narrowing, Reid wondered if she was meeting someone at the creek. Caroline or Kirk? He was inclined to put his money on the latter. Caroline's name hadn't come up since last week. And telling Sammi she couldn't date this boy, *ever,* even after she turned sixteen, had prompted a storm of tears and proclamations of undying, desperate love. Since then she had mooned around the house, scribbling in a notebook. Love poems, Reid had supposed. And now, in direct defiance of his orders, she was probably meeting Kirk down at the creek, exactly where Caroline had said she saw them together last week.

Why would she take a chance on being caught? Because Sammi thought her dear, old, dupable dad was going to be in the lower pasture for most of the morning. So while Dad was working his butt off, why not sneak out to meet the boy he had told you to stay away from?

Flexing his sore fingers and smiling grimly, Reid watched her disappear down the path. He gave her just about enough time to reach the swimming hole, then tugged on his cap and followed. On the one hand, he wanted to be wrong, wanted to believe she was just going for a swim, that she wouldn't defy him this way. On the other hand, he relished the thought of confronting the young smart aleck who was encouraging this behavior. He would put the fear of God into young Mr. Williams, who wouldn't be sniffing around Sammi after this.

Full of righteous indignation, Reid crashed down the final few steps of the path and into the clearing beside the swimming hole. Two people looked up, eyes wide with surprise.

One was Sammi.

The other was Caroline.

Caroline, who wore a jade green bikini that was little more than two strips of stretchy knit that emphasized rather than covered the swell of her breasts and the flare of her hips. Caroline, whose hair was twisted up and away from her face, revealing her long, graceful neck and slender shoulders that had been warmed to a honeyed tan by the sun.

Caroline, whom he didn't want to want, but who made his body stir and harden.

Caroline, in whose eyes he saw a flash of the same emotions he was feeling.

Reid had only one thought, which was more like a prayer. *Dear God, save us both from these basic, biological urges.*

Chapter Four

Caroline had known she shouldn't wear this bathing suit. It wasn't her style. This was made for sunbathing, more suitable for Caribbean resorts than Tennessee creeks. But she and Lainey had spent part of the July 4th weekend shopping in nearby Chattanooga, and while encouraging her cousin to buy something a little more flattering than her customary worn jeans and men's shirts, Caroline had been roped into several frivolous purchases, including this suit.

Why she had worn it out of the privacy of her house was another matter. It had been a lark, an impulse, perhaps an attempt to shake off the inertia that had claimed her for the past week. She thought no one but Sammi or Lainey would see her. Certainly she had never expected Reid McClure, famous for his nose-to-the-grindstone mentality, to come down to the swimming hole on a workday morning.

But here he was. Standing tall and straight. And those dark, unfathomable eyes of his were taking her in, *all* of her. Not lewdly. Just... openly. It required plenty of self-restraint not to fold her hands across her bosom in a feeble attempt at camouflage. Instead she snatched up her T-shirt coverup.

While Caroline pulled that on, Sammi broke the silence. "Dad, what are you doing here?"

"Tractor broke down again." He blinked a few times, pulled off his cap and cleared the perspiration off his face with the back of his forearm before shifting his gaze to Sammi. "What are *you* doing here?"

She lifted her chin. "Caroline's reading my stuff."

"Your stuff?" Once more, those dark eyes of his skipped back to Caroline, touching her briefly, moving on as if he was afraid to linger.

"I like to encourage young writers," she began rather feebly.

A line appeared between his eyebrows. "Young writers?"

Sammi went to her father's side and took his arm. "Dad, I told you I thought I wanted to be a writer." She sighed dramatically, then gave him a brilliant smile, as if a great problem had been solved. "Well, now I'm sure."

But her melodrama seemed to bemuse rather than impress her father. "Last month you wanted to be an astronaut."

"I wanted to be an astronaut when I was in fifth grade."

"Then maybe last month it was an oceanologist."

Dropping his arm, Sammi flounced away. "You never listen to me."

"Perhaps I should go," Caroline interrupted, edging toward the water.

But Sammi protested, "You promised to look at what I've been working on."

Resisting her appeal was difficult. Caroline looked back at Reid. "I didn't think you'd mind my talking to Sammi about this," she murmured. "We met down here again a few days ago—"

"By accident," Sammi put in.

Caroline nodded. "I listened to part of a short story she's been writing. She asked me to help her. I said I would, if you agreed. I wasn't about to encourage her to disobey you, not after last week." Now she sent a reproving look in the girl's direction. "Sammi told me you said this was okay."

Reid's expression grew thunderous as he regarded his daughter. "Lying seems to be Sammi's way of dealing with everything these days."

The teenager crossed her arms, her face set in sullen lines. "I knew you'd just say no."

"You're supposed to be grounded."

"Grounded from going anywhere with my friends."

"From doing anything I've asked you not to do."

"But this isn't like play or anything," Sammi protested. "Writing is hard work."

"Please—"

"Reid," Caroline cut in, "don't be angry with Sammi. This is my fault. I should have known she didn't get your permission. I guess I just thought that

after the other night when you and I...when we..."
She hesitated, not knowing exactly how to describe
what had passed between them last week. "Talked"
seemed far too innocuous a description.

"Yes," Reid said, clearing his throat. "The other
night..." But he, too, didn't seem to know what he was
trying to say.

Before Caroline could continue, she noticed the
sharpening interest in Sammi's regard, the obviously
speculative gleam in her eyes as her gaze moved from
Caroline to Reid and back again. Sammi was quite
perceptive. But then, a person could be dense and still
pick up on the undercurrents at work here. Sammi had
to have noticed the way her father had looked at Caroline when he'd stepped into the clearing, and the way
neither of them could look at the other now.

Not wanting to fuel an overactive imagination, Caroline made herself look Reid squarely in the eye and
keep her voice level. "After you and I had our little
discussion the other night, I thought you might not be
so opposed to me spending time with Sammi. But perhaps I should have called and checked it out with you."

She would have called, she thought, if she hadn't felt
like such a fool the morning after the episode at her
house. If she hadn't been so unnerved by what had
passed between the two of them. If he hadn't roused
feelings she thought she didn't possess. But with all of
that to consider, it had been easier to accept what
Sammi told her than to pick up the phone and check it
out with Reid. She had thought it best to avoid him altogether.

"I'm not opposed," Reid said now. He looked as if his own words took him by surprise, but he went on, "What I mean to say is that it's okay if you and Sammi spend some time together."

Heaving a relieved sigh, Sammi began, "If I'd have known that—"

Reid stopped her with an upraised hand, his expression hardening again. "I don't object. But you should have told me. I thought after I caught you sneaking out last week that you'd realize you can't just keep doing whatever you want to do, any old time you want to do it."

"I know, I know," Sammi said, rolling her eyes. "Dad, we've already *done* this lecture."

"How about if you *do* another week's worth of grounding?"

The suggestion sparked the beginning of another protest, but a warning look from Reid quickly silenced Sammi. Caroline couldn't help but feel some sympathy for the girl, but she was disappointed in her, too.

Days ago, when they had run into each other again, Caroline had apologized for having to reveal Sammi's meeting with Kirk to Reid. She explained, however, that she wouldn't have made that promise if she had known how opposed Reid was to Sammi seeing Kirk. Something in Sammi's careless manner made Caroline suspicious. She wouldn't doubt the girl was still finding ways to meet her boyfriend. Caroline made it clear that she wouldn't cover Sammi's tracks. If she saw her with Kirk, she'd have to tell Reid. That honest and above-board approach had been accepted by Sammi, but then she had been less than forthright with Caroline in return.

As if he was thinking the same thing, Reid said, "Sammi, I think you owe Caroline an apology."

The girl looked up, frowning. "Caroline?"

"Because you lied to her, too, about clearing this with me."

Long, dark curls swung forward as Sammi again bowed her head. "I'm sorry," she murmured. "I guess this is it for you helping me with my story, isn't it?"

Caroline shrugged. "That's up to your father."

"We'll talk after you're no longer grounded," Reid said.

"Dad—"

"Don't push it, Cookie."

The nickname Reid used took the sting out of his words. A long look, full of resolve but tempered by strong affection, passed between father and daughter. Finally, Reid teasingly tugged the end of one of his daughter's spiraling curls. She rolled her eyes, but gave him a grudging grin.

Caroline knew a moment's envy. No one had ever loved her in this easy, unqualified way. Not her troubled mother. Certainly not the father who had left her. Not her grandfather or husband.

Her twin brother might have, if he had lived. Perhaps that was why her one treasured photograph of Adam had given her such sweet comfort over the years. Perhaps the peace that picture brought her was the reason she often thought he must be alive somewhere. That old, familiar wish brought a fleeting smile to her lips.

"Isn't that right, Caroline?"

Realizing Sammi had spoken, she glanced up. "Excuse me?"

"I have to go hear the speech you're giving at the library tomorrow afternoon, don't I?"

Caroline looked from the girl's eager face to Reid. He said Sammi was grounded, and she wasn't about to argue with that. "It's not really a speech, Sammi."

"But you're going to talk about what it's like to be a writer, aren't you?"

In all honesty, Caroline wasn't sure what she would talk about. She had agreed to speak at the local library's monthly community tea during her first week home, when she had been riding high from the exhilaration of her reunion with Lainey and the beginning of her search for the key to her locked memory. Since then, she had lost her enthusiasm for the event. Lost her enthusiasm for anything, really. She wasn't even writing. Every word of the new book brought on the same sort of crippling fear she had first experienced that night in Lainey's kitchen just before Reid had come looking for Sammi. Her memories were waiting for her, but she now suspected they were far more horrible than she had ever imagined.

Lately she wondered if remembering was really what she wanted.

With little help from Caroline, Sammi was still appealing to her father for permission to attend the library event. "I know I'm still grounded, but I just have to go. It's not like going to the movies or anything. It'll be educational."

"I don't know if I'd go that far," Caroline said.

But Sammi ignored her. "You could go, too, Dad."

Reid glanced at Caroline, then away, and murmured something about being busy.

"But I've always said you'd love Caroline's books," his daughter insisted. "Even before we met her." She was grinning and glancing from her father to Caroline and back again in a way that made Caroline nervous.

"Don't you have some chores to do?" Reid cut in.

Sammi wheedled, "If I do the chores, can I go?"

"If you don't do them . . ." Reid retorted with heavy meaning.

The teenager's grin turned into an outright giggle. She grabbed up her canvas tote and started up the path, calling over her shoulder, "*We'll* see you tomorrow, Caroline!"

She was gone before Reid could reply, and the clearing beside the creek was suddenly silent.

Caroline managed to find her voice first. "She's quite a ball of fire, your daughter."

"These days she's just one big ball of trouble."

"Oh, I think it's just natural high spirits . . ." Caroline tried to choke back the words and managed a short laugh. "I promised myself I wasn't going to offer you any more advice about your daughter."

"Why is that?" Turning his back to her, Reid set his cap and water jug down on a rock at the water's edge and pulled a handkerchief from his back pocket.

As he knelt on the rock, Caroline reflected that many women would enjoy this particular view of Reid McClure's physique. She tried to tell herself she wasn't one of them, while she told him, "You don't want my advice."

"You're smart to realize that." Worn denim stretched tight over his firm behind and broad shoulders strained his blue chambray shirt as he leaned over and dipped the handkerchief in the water.

"Yet you're letting her spend time with me."

Reid wrapped the handkerchief around the fingers on his left hand. "Better you than Kirk Williams." He flexed his fingers and grimaced before she could comment.

"What's the matter?" she asked.

He stood and faced her, holding up his injured hand. "Burned it on the tractor's radiator."

"Water won't do much for a burn. You need some ice and some medicated salve or aloe."

"Do you see any of those around?" he retorted gruffly, wincing. "The water makes it feel better."

Caroline glanced at the handkerchief. "That thing is filthy." Without thinking, and over his protests, she took his hand in her own and peeled off the dingy-looking cloth. The burned area was a bright, angry red, with a blister already beginning to form. "This looks terrible."

"It'll be okay."

"But you shouldn't wrap it in this nasty thing."

"Caroline—"

"I don't have anything cleaner for you to wrap it in but my T-shirt." Dropping his hand, she bent over to examine the hem of the nearly knee-length garment. "Maybe if I ripped off an edge—"

"Don't."

The roughness of that one muttered word made her look up and into his eyes. They were narrow slits, matched by the lines that bracketed his mouth.

"Don't," he repeated. "Don't bother your T-shirt. Don't rip it. Don't take it off."

The intensity of his regard reminded her of her scanty bathing suit and how he had looked at her when he'd come down the path. Flushing, she stepped back.

But that was as far as she moved. They stood as they were, their gazes locked, the air between them simmering with awareness.

Caroline couldn't take it for long. She had to say something, anything, to break the spell. "You should..." Her voice faltered, then steadied. "You should definitely put something on that burn as soon as you get back to the house."

"I will."

"And I'll just go." She pointed over her shoulder, to a spot somewhere up the path. But she didn't leave. She just started to babble, desperately, because she needed to fill this tense, charged silence. "I waded the creek upstream and crossed over to the path on your side. The water was up over my ankles. There's been so much rain this summer. It was like this my last summer here, when Kevin and I..."

His brother's name set Reid in motion. "Yeah," he muttered, turning away. "Just like that summer." With tight, jerky movements, he picked up his water jug and pulled on his cap. "See you," he offered before setting off.

Caroline knew the wisest course of action was to let him go. But something about Reid McClure robbed her of whatever wisdom she had accumulated in this life.

"I thought we were over this," she said quietly, just as Reid reached the start of the path.

He turned back toward her. Reluctantly, she thought. "Over what?"

"This thing between us about Kevin."

He didn't reply, and the brim of his cap shaded his eyes so that she couldn't read his expression.

"Even if I am just the lesser of two evils, I hoped your decision to let me spend some time with Sammi meant you had revised your opinion about my supposed influence on Kevin."

The only clue to Reid's reaction was the thinning line of his mouth. His voice was flat, emotionless. "Maybe you and I should agree not to discuss my brother, all right?"

"But, Reid—"

"Listen, Caroline." He walked toward her again. "If Sammi wants to talk to you, I'm going to let her, because I'd rather save my fights with her for the bigger stuff."

"And Kirk Williams is bigger?"

"I think so."

"So you don't trust Sammi to stay away from him?"

"I trust that randy little rich boy a whole lot less."

Caroline shook her head. "If Sammi wants to be with him, she'll find a way, you know." She tilted her chin. "Kevin and I did."

He stepped close enough that she could see his eyes again. "I'm counting on you not to use what you and Kevin once did to encourage Sammi with Kirk."

"I told you last week that I wasn't out to cause any trouble for you or your daughter. Now that I know how much you dislike this boy, I wouldn't dream of interfering."

"Good." He turned to go.

But Caroline stopped him once more. "Maybe I'm slow or something, but I'm still a little confused about this. You now trust me enough to believe I won't influence Sammi with this boy, but you still blame me for what happened to Kevin?"

Reid hesitated to give her an answer. Perhaps because he was just as confused as she was. He had held on to his hatred of this woman for so many years that it was difficult to accept any change in his assumptions about her. Just an hour or so ago, he had reminded himself that she was a Parrish and therefore not to be trusted. But then he had given her carte blanche with his daughter. It didn't make sense. He wasn't making sense. He shouldn't trust Caroline Parrish *or* Kirk Williams with Sammi. But standing here, looking at her, he kept forgetting that she was an enemy.

"Aren't you afraid I'll fill Sammi's head with nonsense?" she pressed, as if determined to remind him he was being foolish. "I mean, Heaven forbid, she might actually want to become something as frivolous as a writer. She might leave here—"

"She probably will."

"What?"

"She'll leave," Reid said, although he wondered why he was compelled to explain himself to her. "I'll want her to leave. But only when she's ready."

"And you'll decide that, I guess."

Ignoring her sarcasm, he went on, "I'll want her to leave for the right reasons."

"So Kevin left for the wrong ones?"

"Yes."

"It must be nice to always be so sure of what's right."

Reid doffed his hat, once again clearing the perspiration from his forehead with his arm. "You know something? I've got about a hundred things I should be doing instead of standing around in the noonday sun while you try to pick a fight with me. Let's just lay it to rest about my brother, all right?"

"I'm not trying to fight. I've just always wondered how it felt to be like you."

"Like me?"

Her ebony gaze swept over him, devoid of the sarcasm he expected. "To have everything come so easily."

He didn't know what in the hell she was talking about. "Excuse me?"

"I think it comes from always having known exactly who you are."

Disgusted, he fitted his cap back on his head. "I hear people say all the time that they don't know who they are. But I happen to think that's just a bunch of bull to keep psychiatrists in business."

"That's not fair. Not everyone is born into the sort of security you and Kevin had."

"Security?" he repeated, not following her logic. "Aren't you forgetting a few things? Like how damned hard it was for our father to beat a living out of this land? He died when he was younger than I am now. Then Mother was gone, too, and me and Kevin were completely alone. Is that security to you?"

She made an impatient, sweeping motion with her hands. "I'm not talking about any of that. I'm talking about the way you feel about yourself. The security of being at ease in your own skin. Kevin had it, too—that same self-confidence. He just wanted something so different from life that you couldn't understand or accept his decisions."

There was truth in her words that Reid didn't want to confront, the same truth she had tossed at him every time his brother's name came up. He reacted with his customary shield of anger. "I thought we weren't going to talk about Kevin."

Caroline regarded him in silence for a few moments before agreeing, "You're right. We weren't going to discuss him again. I'm sorry." She turned away, seeking out her beach towel and bag and with quick, nervous movements. "I'm sorry I rambled on like that. I guess it's just that I always envied Kev—" She caught herself. "I envied your family."

"Envied us?" Reid repeated. It was hard to imagine that someone growing up in the Parrish mansion would envy the struggling McClures. Certainly her family's fortune had been depleted by the time Caroline was born, but it hadn't been gone. From his side of the creek, the side without the big house or the expensive cars, she had appeared to have most everything she wanted as a child. "What did we ever have that you would envy?"

"It's just what I was trying to say a minute ago," Caroline said, her back still to him. "You and Kevin, you had this confidence, this surety that everything would turn out okay." She turned to look at him now, her eyes troubled. "I never had that security. And I wanted...it." Her voice broke on the last word and she looked away again, hurriedly stuffing her towel into her bag.

Reid studied her sleek, bowed head with concern. "Caroline, is everything—"

"Everything's fine," she cut in, her voice once more under control, though she didn't look up at him. "I'm just out of sorts today. I'm just...just thinking about not staying the rest of the summer."

He should have been glad, but he wasn't. And he refused to dwell on the reasons why. "Then you figured out what it was you needed to know?"

"You mean, did I remember what happened the night Mother died?" Her laughter was short and clipped, lacking humor. "No."

"But you're going home just the same?"

She looked at him then, with a smile that didn't reach her eyes. "This valley is my home, Reid. I knew it the moment I saw the farm again. This is home, but I don't think I can stay."

"Don't think? You mean, you're not sure?"

"No, I'm not," she retorted. "I'm not like you. I've never known where I belonged or who I was or exactly what I should do. I've never been . . . safe."

Safe? He wondered at her choice of words. But then, thinking of her as she had been last week, of the terror in her eyes and the way her slim body had trembled in his arms, he supposed she didn't feel safe. Not with a memory that had turned traitor. Not when panic could take her on a dark ride. What had happened to her? What in God's name had her grandfather done to inspire a fear that had lasted this long? Those questions sent fury curling through Reid's gut. Fury and a strong, protective urge.

She attempted another smile as she slipped her bag over one shoulder. She murmured a hurried "Goodbye," then brushed past him, headed for the path.

Reid should have let her pass. He definitely should *not* have put out his hand, caught her elbow so that she had no choice but to face him.

"Caroline," he began, although he had no idea what it was he wanted to say to her. But he repeated her name.

"Yes?"

Somehow he forced his voice around the frog in his throat. He said the words he shouldn't say, not even to himself. "Don't leave."

Her eyes widened. "What?"

He cleared his throat again. "Just don't."

"But why?"

Because he couldn't give voice to his real reason, he said the first thing he thought of. "You'll regret it. All the rest of your life, you'll regret leaving here not knowing what you came to find out."

"But I'm not sure I can handle what my mind decided I should forget. Maybe that's the whole reason I forgot. Because it was all more than I could stand." She bit her lower lip, a movement that made him focus on her mouth. Her sweetly tempting, full mouth. Try as he might, he couldn't look away.

"I'm afraid," she whispered.

"Will running away stop that fear?"

"I don't know."

"Did it stop it before?"

"No, but—"

"Then stay."

"I shouldn't."

"Stay," he whispered.

As if drawn by an invisible thread, Caroline swayed toward him. He knew he shouldn't, but he raised his hand and tucked a few wayward, silky tendrils of hair behind her ear. He didn't want to draw her closer, yet he had to. He tried with every fiber of his being to resist the invitation in her eyes and on her lush, parted lips. But he failed. Miserably.

So he kissed her.

As kisses went, it was pretty innocent. Just a soft melding. A gentle quest. It shouldn't have set a fire inside him, shouldn't have tightened his body into full arousal, shouldn't have provoked thoughts of a deeper, more intimate joining. Except for his hand in her hair and his mouth against hers, he didn't touch her. And yet the moment for him was totally, completely erotic.

He didn't know what Caroline thought. She didn't stick around long enough for him to gauge her reaction. She drew away from him and left the clearing without looking at him again, without looking back.

And he just stood in the sun, aching for her.

This was more than your basic, biological urge.

Reid wasn't sure how long he stayed by the creek, kicking himself for his foolishness and yet replaying that kiss in his mind. It was long past noon when he finally walked into the kitchen at home. His daughter studied him for a moment and looked at the clock, her eyebrow raised. That's when Reid realized his daughter was on to his attraction to Caroline.

For the rest of that day and on into the next morning, he avoided Sammi as much as possible. He was quite sure that if she looked hard enough, she would be able to see that he couldn't get Caroline out of his head. He wanted to put thoughts of her aside. He wanted to forget he had ever touched her. He told himself to be happy she was leaving. But that wasn't possible.

God help him, all he could think about was seeing her, touching her again.

At lunch the next day, he casually asked Sammi what time Caroline would be speaking at the library.

"Oh, three o'clock or so," was her blithe reply as she handed him a plate of sliced home-grown tomatoes.

Reid speared a few for his sandwich and avoided his daughter's gaze. "Since I've got to go into town and pick up some things at the hardware store, I guess I'll take you by the library."

"Thanks, Dad." Sammi bounced out of her chair and dropped a kiss on his cheek. "Why don't you come, too?"

He kept his shrug deliberately offhand. "We'll see."

Sammi didn't reply, didn't wheedle or whine. That surprised him so much that he glanced up. He was just in time to catch a distinctly satisfied grin on her face.

He waited for a smart-ass comment, but "Whatever you say" was all she offered.

He relaxed.

And that's when she hit him. "You should wear your black jeans, Dad." Her smile could have lit up a room. "They do nice things for your buns."

She wisely dashed out of the room before Reid could sputter a reply.

But that afternoon at three-thirty, when he slipped into the public library, he was wearing black denim.

From the podium where she stood, Caroline caught Reid's entry into the library's community room. Momentarily, the passage she was reading swam before her eyes. But she gathered her composure and forged ahead, pleased that her voice didn't shake.

"'They were two,'" she read. "'Two joined in the womb, but held by the bonds, the curse, of their gift. She was fair, straight and slim, with eyes that were bluer than the Mycoglian sea at high tide. He was dark, shorter and stouter, with midnight captured in his gaze. From birth, they both knew their place. They would be saviors to a dying race. But neither guessed the agony or the danger of that quest.

"'Their adventure began with the rumor of his death.'"

Smiling, Caroline closed the book, then looked up at her audience, careful to avoid Reid's gaze. "That's the way I began my first book. And like the story of

Princess Mai and Prince Moren, my career has been
quite an adventure.''

She went on to make some lighthearted remarks
about rejected manuscripts, eventual publication and
the reaction of fans. When she was through, she
opened the floor to questions from the audience and
was pleased when so many hands shot into the air. Actually, she was astounded by the entire event. The room
was packed, something she hadn't expected given that
it was a workday afternoon. Sammi and a group of her
friends were in the front row. Lainey was behind her.
Men, women, old friends and strangers were scattered
throughout the sea of faces. But only one stood out.

Reid.

As she waded through the questions, she was con-
stantly aware of his intense, dark-eyed regard. He
seemed changed today. Older. Maybe it was his clothes.
His white cotton button-down wasn't so very different
than the blue work shirts that were his usual garb, but
the crisp color emphasized his deep tan. Yet perhaps
the change was something much less superficial. Maybe
it had to do with her perceptions. Possibly, it had everything to do with her memory of his unexpected kiss.

The feel of his firm, warm lips was as clear to her
now as the moment they had touched her own. So was
her reaction. She had wanted to stay. To put her arms
around him. To draw him deeper into the kiss. That
was the reason she had run away. Because she wanted
so much more than just that one caress. Never had she
wanted a man's touch the way she wanted Reid Mc-
Clure's. And, quite frankly, she didn't know what to do
with these new desires and sensations. So she had fled.

She had hoped that a little more time would elapse before she saw him again. She thought she would eventually forget the feelings he had sent coursing through her. But she knew now that she was wrong.

Because she wanted him to kiss her again.

After nearly two decades of avoiding kisses, she couldn't stop wondering about the hows, whens and wheres of the next one. It was astounding. Especially since it was Reid McClure she wanted to kiss.

Out of all the men in the world. *Reid McClure.*

Later, Caroline couldn't guess how she made it through the final half of the question-and-answer session. Her gaze kept straying in Reid's direction, then slipping away. She was so sure he would be able to see what she was thinking, what she was wanting.

Afterward, she was whisked out of the community room and into the front parlor of the restored Victorian home that housed the library. There, over tea and cookies, Caroline had to play meet-and-greet, shaking hands and answering questions for those who had been too shy to talk from the floor. The crowd ebbed and flowed around her, but she kept looking in vain for the one face she had avoided up until now.

Sammi came up, her friends in tow, obviously pleased that she was able to claim friendship with a real live author. Caroline indulged her, even complimented Sammi's own writing.

Glowing from the praise, the teenager said, "Did you see that Dad came?" A titter ran through her assembled cohorts. She sent them a warning glance.

Caroline fought not to flush. She felt as goofy and awkward as these girls, who were all long limbs and blemishes and braces. She could practically feel their leaping hormones and tried not to feed off their nerves.

"I saw your dad," she told Sammi calmly. "He slipped in a little late."

"He looks cool, don't you think?"

"Cool? I . . . I guess."

Again, the youthful laughter bubbled up. Again, Sammi quelled it with a tilt of her head. But she didn't have a chance to say anything. Sammi's father appeared at her side, and for Caroline, everyone else in the room simply ceased to exist.

He did look cool, she thought. The white shirt topped off neatly pressed black denim jeans. They molded his long, sturdy legs with the sort of fit a clothing designer might only dream of for the models in the advertisements placed in upscale magazines. And yet Reid had none of the pretty-boy good looks of any model Caroline had ever seen. He was rugged. Big and brawny. His body had been built by hard work. The lines on his face, which she imagined would fascinate most photographers, had been earned by days in the sun and wind. There were some people who wouldn't care for his rough edges. She liked them fine.

"Reid," she said, hoping she didn't sound as nervous as she felt.

"Caroline." Did she imagine it, or was his voice deeper, hoarser than usual?

"I didn't expect you to come," she told him.

His glance strayed to his daughter. "I guess this is good practice for when my daughter is a famous novelist."

With practiced ease, Sammi flipped a strand of hair over her shoulder. "Lame, Dad. Really lame."

"Don't tell me you've changed your career aspirations again in the last twenty-four hours."

Sammi's peanut gallery laughed, a little too freely, Caroline thought. While Reid was distracted by all that noise and attention, Sammi shifted gears as easily, as quickly as anyone Caroline had ever seen. Her smile was brilliant as, with just the right amount of casualness, she asked Reid, "Is it okay if I go spend the night with Loni? Her mom said she'd bring me home in the morning."

Just as smoothly, Reid replied, "Sure. But come home early."

The girls melted away, barely sparing goodbyes for Caroline, who laughed.

Reid looked surprised. "What is it?"

"Nothing, except isn't Sammi supposed to be grounded?"

His head whipped around, but Sammi and her friends had disappeared. His expression made Caroline laugh even harder.

"It's the old gang-up routine," he grumbled. "She knows it works every time."

"'Gang-up'?"

"She gets all those girls together, asks for something she knows she shouldn't, but knows I'll probably give in. She's been pulling that since she was in first grade."

"She's one smart cookie."

He grinned. "That's how she got her nickname."

"I wondered about that," Caroline said, feeling suddenly and unbelievably at ease with him.

He smiled at her, almost shyly, she thought. And then he drew her over to the side of the room, away from the crowd that had broken up into smaller groups.

"Listen," he began. "I wonder if—"

He was cut off by a man who approached Caroline's other side. She looked up, irritated, when the man touched her arm.

"Caroline," he said.

And the world fell out from under her.

He repeated her name and held out his hand. But she couldn't reply, certainly couldn't conjure the strength to shake his hand.

All at once she wasn't standing in the library. She was lying on the cold, wet ground, with rain streaming over her. A stranger was bending close, saying her name. When she tried to answer, she tasted blood.

"Caroline."

Reid's voice penetrated the fog and the rain that had risen to claim her from some hole in her past. She reached out, caught the hand he offered. She concentrated on his hand, his strength, and the world that had been fading in front of her eyes came once more into sharp focus.

But the face in front of her, the face of the man who had touched her arm, was the same as the face from the dream.

"Sheriff Leavitt," she managed to choke out.

He smiled, and she wanted to scream.

Chapter Five

Caroline managed, just barely, to stifle her cry.

Sheriff Tatum Leavitt, tall and rangy, with a shock of thick white hair crowning his head, regarded her with concern. "Caroline, you're pale as can be."

"I'm sorry, I—"

Still gripping her hand, Reid guided her toward a group of chairs that lined the wall. "I think you need to sit down."

She took a seat while the sheriff pressed a cup of tea on her. "You need this more than I do," he said, and sat down beside her.

She mumbled a thank-you and took a deep gulp of the warm, sweet liquid. Then she closed her eyes and gathered her thoughts before looking at Leavitt again. Now that she saw him clearly, she realized he had changed in the past seventeen years. The hair was thinner, the lines in his face deeper and his eyebrows even more bristling than before. "I'm sorry. It's just that the last time I saw you—"

"Was in the hospital," the older man supplied. Regret flickered in his faded blue eyes. "It was after the accident. I came up to talk to you about it after you regained consciousness. You were still confused. Got all upset because you couldn't remember what happened." He looked up at Reid, who was standing at her side. "I guess that's why seeing me set her back for a minute."

She shook her head. "I don't mean I remember you from the hospital. I'm talking about right after the accident. Right there, on the scene. You were there, weren't you?"

"We were shorthanded that night. I had to take a patrol myself, and I just happened along right after it happened." He shook his head, clucking slightly. "It was terrible. Just terrible."

"I remember you bending over me, talking to me."

Sheriff Leavitt gave her a sympathetic look. "You didn't come to at the accident, Caroline. I remember, because I was scared senseless we were going to lose you, too."

"But I remember you being there," she insisted.

"Maybe I told you I was there. Or your grandfather told you—"

"No," she denied emphatically. "He never told me anything."

The sheriff frowned. "I don't know. You might have had a lucid minute or two, after the ambulance got there and they went to work on you. Maybe that's when you saw me."

"You were bending over me..." She closed her eyes. Once more she saw him, felt the rain, smelled the mud, tasted the blood on her lips. And there was more, something she had tried to tell him.

Reid touched her shoulder. "Caroline, are you all right?"

She said she was, but that was a lie. In reality, she felt as if she could fly apart. Shatter into a thousand tiny pieces. Damn it, she remembered this man, remembered the way he had bent over her, the fear and panic in his voice.

"You called my name again and again," she said to Leavitt. "You told me to hold on, not to die."

His friendly concern had given way to a wariness. He patted Caroline's hand, the way someone pats a child or a mental case. "You shouldn't think about it. It was tragic, just a tragic, awful night. I'm sorry I reminded you of it. All I really wanted was to say hello and welcome you home." He got up and moved away, clearly eager to get away from her.

"This'll be good for a story down at his office," Caroline muttered.

Reid took the seat the older man had vacated. "What'll be good?"

"Me. Crazy Caroline Parrish. He'll have something to tell his officers."

"He doesn't have any officers. He retired a few years back."

But Caroline barely heard him. She was thinking of the accident again, of the rain in her face, and of how hard she had tried to speak to Sheriff Leavitt. What had she tried to tell him?

The touch of Reid's hand on her arm brought her attention back to the present. "Are you really okay?"

"I remember him," she said. "I know I remember him, Reid. Do you think he'd have some reason to lie to me?"

Reid shook his head, slowly, his gaze filled with genuine concern.

She sighed and dragged a hand through her hair. "You're right. What possible reason would he have to lie about this?"

"But you think you remember him."

"I don't think. I *know* he was there."

"It was a long time ago. Maybe you're really just remembering when he came to the hospital."

She didn't buy that. "That's not it."

Reid would have pressed her some more, pushed her to remember more, but this was neither the time nor place for that.

The crowd had rediscovered Caroline. More people were demanding a moment of her time. The director of the library took her off to pose for a picture for the local paper. Reid thought what she needed was to leave, to go somewhere and get her bearings, take a deep breath and get some color back in her cheeks. Before Sheriff Leavitt had interrupted, Reid had been about to ask Caroline to go have some dinner with him.

Yes, *dinner*.

A *date*.

With Caroline Parrish.

That thought made his head hurt. Or maybe the headache came from this small room with all these loud people who had turned out to get a look at the long, lost Parrish, the final member of the county's founding family. Reid wondered how many of the people who were once again crowding around Caroline actually gave a hoot about any of the books she had written. Of course, he was a fine one to talk. It wasn't an interest in literature that had brought him here.

He was curious about what these people thought of her. In her white ruffled blouse and long, brightly colored skirt, she looked out of place among the pastel suits and pearls most of the women wore. The little bit of leg he could see beneath the skirt hem was tanned and bare with red-tipped toes showing through low-heeled sandals. Her hair was smoothed back behind her ears, bangs feathering her forehead. Silver earrings swung forward against the honeyed tan of her neck. She looked exotic. Like a wild rose taken root among a bed of hothouse flowers.

He didn't want to just sit here, staring at her. So he got to his feet and threaded his way through the crowd. No one said much to him. He imagined a couple of the people he nodded to were wondering what in the hell he was doing there. Library teas weren't his normal domain.

Outside on the library's broad front porch, he took in a couple of deep breaths of fresh air. Then he settled off to the side and watched people stream out of the building for nearly half an hour. But not Caroline.

He finally went in search of her. The place was once more as quiet as he would expect it to be. Only a couple of women bustled about, clearing the tea table in the front parlor.

He stopped the director in front of the circulation desk. "Is Caroline still here?"

"She left about ten minutes ago."

"I didn't see her leave."

"I believe she had parked out back."

Her car wasn't in the parking lot behind the building. She was gone.

Since he had never actually gotten around to asking her to have dinner, Reid knew he shouldn't feel slighted. But he did. The least she could have done was seek him out to say goodbye. Maybe she had tried and not found him. And maybe she had been back in her natural element here, with all these people her family used to hobnob with when she was a girl, and it hadn't occurred to her to look for him. For all he knew, she was out to dinner with one of the town's leading citizens.

Grumbling, he got in his truck and headed for home. By the time he reached the city limits, he was telling himself it was probably for the best that she had left. He had been saved from a bad mistake. He'd had no business kissing her. Asking her to dinner would have been an impulsive mistake. But just for a minute there, when they had laughed together over Sammi's maneuvering tactics, he had forgotten who she was, what she represented to him. He should thank his lucky stars that she had gone out the back way.

He was so busy trying to convince himself that he preferred a cold dinner alone at home to one with Caroline, he almost missed her car. It was in the curve, just before the entrance to Applewood, well off the road. The nose was in the ditch. The rear tires were tilted off the ground.

He passed it, swore, then hit his brakes too hard and skidded, coming close to the ditch himself. Leaving his truck running, he sprinted back up the road. Over the pounding of his heart, he could hear her car's engine grinding, as if someone was trying to start it. Calling her name, he waded into the brush and the mud of the ditch and wrenched open her driver's door.

Caroline was there. White and shaking, one hand gripping the steering wheel while the other kept turning the key in the ignition. Her foot was pumping the gas pedal.

"Stop it," Reid told her. "Stop trying to start it!"

She gave him a blank look, so he just leaned across her and jerked the keys away. "Caroline, what are you trying to do?"

When she still didn't reply, he took hold of her arms and half dragged, half carried her out of the car and the ditch and out onto the road. She sagged against him, and he allowed himself a moment, just one moment, of clutching her tight against him and breathing a relieved prayer.

Then he drew away and stared down into her tear-streaked face. "God Almighty, woman, what happened?"

All she said was, "I remembered."

Then she stepped back into his arms and held on, held him as though she would never let him go.

They were still standing that way when Lainey's pickup truck came around the curve.

* * *

"You need to eat something."

Turning from the front window of her house, Caroline looked at Lainey. The redhead was carrying a tray loaded with coffee and sandwiches in from the kitchen. Enough sandwiches to feed ten people.

Caroline managed a shaky laugh. "Why it is that when something bad happens, we always start making food?"

Lainey set the tray down on the old trunk in front of the sofa. "'Feed the good times, feed the sad,' was what Aunt Loretta used to say."

"She was always feeding somebody, wasn't she?" Sitting down on the sofa, Caroline kicked off her sandals and then accepted the mug of coffee handed to her. "I remember after I had been gone from here for a while, the mother of one of the women I worked with passed away. I showed up at her door with a meal I had cooked. You know, just like we always did back here. If someone died, you made a dish or two and carried it over to the house. This friend of mine and her family had never heard of such a thing." She sighed and took a sip of her coffee. "But as I recall, they made short work of Aunt Loretta's chicken and rice casscasserole."

The way her voice broke on the last word brought Lainey to her side. She perched on the arm of the sofa and put her arm around Caroline. "Are you sure you shouldn't go in and get checked over?"

"My seat belt was on. I didn't hit my head or anything else. I'm fine, just fine."

"But it was frightening just the same."

"Yes, yes it was." After drinking a little more coffee, Caroline reached for one of the sandwiches, even though she didn't know how she would choke it down. "These look good, Lainey."

As she might have expected, the other woman didn't press for more details about what had happened. She hadn't asked many questions since pulling to a stop beside Caroline and Reid out on the road. Together, Lainey and Reid had put Caroline in Lainey's truck. On the way to the house, she had stopped by the barn and sent her farmhand to help Reid get the car out of the ditch. Since then, Caroline had said very little, certainly nothing about what she had remembered, and Lainey hadn't asked any questions.

"I wonder why it's taking so long," Caroline murmured, putting the barely touched sandwich down and going back to the window. Outside, the summer sun lingered, but the shadows were beginning to creep over the ridge behind the farm.

Lainey switched on the lamp on the end table. "They'll be along in a minute or two. I wouldn't think it would be too complicated to get the car out."

She was right. Caroline's car, followed by Reid's black truck, came over the hill behind the big house not long after that. Her car was fine, Reid reported, handing over the keys when Caroline met him at the door. Just a banged-up front fender and a few scratches.

He gave her a long, assessing look. "I have a feeling the car's better off than you."

"She needs to eat something," Lainey said. "I bet she hasn't had anything since breakfast. She was too nervous about that library talk to have any lunch with me."

"I'm just not hungry."

Reid captured her chin in his hand and made her look straight at him. "You'll feel better if you eat."

"I don't—"

"Caroline." He took hold of her shoulders, slipped his hands down her arms and enfolded her fingers in his. His touch was warm, reassuring. "You're cold as ice. Why don't you sit down and at least have some coffee?"

Seeing the wisdom in that, she turned back to the sofa while Reid excused himself and went to the bathroom to clean off some of the mud from the ditch.

Lainey cleared her throat and stood. "I think I'm what's known as a fifth wheel here."

Caroline protested, "Don't be silly."

"I've got eyes," the redhead retorted. "I could see there was something a little more than neighborly about the way Reid was holding you out there on the road."

"I was upset. And he was there. Anyone—"

But Lainey didn't go for that. "I'm going to take off and let you two talk." She gave Caroline a brief, hard hug. "If you need anything, you holler." With a mischievous grin, she filched one of the sandwiches off the tray and left.

Reid appeared just after the front door closed. "Lainey gone?"

Nodding, Caroline sat down again. She poured Reid a mug of coffee from the insulated pot Lainey had filled. He took it and sat down beside her. Not too close, but comfortably near.

A moment or two of silence passed before he asked, "You want to tell me what happened?"

Though she intended to tell him, she hesitated a moment, refilling her own coffee, then holding the warm mug between her hands, trying to remember and yet wanting to forget what it was that had made her lose control of her car.

Reid wasn't about to let her forget. "What did you remember?"

She let out a sigh and put her coffee aside again. "I feel so stupid, letting some memory run me off the road like that. It shouldn't have happened."

"But it did."

"Yeah." She stood again, suddenly too nervous to sit still. Not looking at Reid, she prowled around the room, silent in her bare feet, pausing by the fireplace mantle, then going to her desk, where she picked up the photograph of her and Adam as children. Turning, she held the framed snapshot out toward Reid, who remained on the couch.

"This is my brother," she told him. "The model for Prince Moren in my books."

Reid took the photograph, studied it for moment, then looked up at her, his confusion clear.

"Do you remember him?" Caroline asked.

He frowned, gazing down at the picture again. Then he shook his head. "I suppose I saw you and him when you were little, but I don't remember it. I was a big boy by the time you came along, not very interested in little kids. And, if you'll recall, there wasn't too much fraternization between our two families."

"Because Grandfather didn't think you were good enough to fraternize with."

"And because he repeatedly tried to buy our place from my grandfather and my father," Reid pointed out. "It infuriated him that they wouldn't sell. Supposedly he wanted to restore Applewood Farm to its original acreage."

Caroline took the picture again and thoughtfully stroked her finger over the glass that covered Adam's features. She wondered what he might have looked like if he had grown up. Like her?

Like their father in the photograph Lainey had dug out of her mother's chest? Caroline had left that picture of her mother and father up at the big house, unsettled by the emotions it evoked.

She looked up as Reid said her name. He had gotten up from the sofa and come around it to stand beside her. He took the picture from her again, then set it aside. "What's this got to do with what you remembered today?"

Caroline took a deep breath and plunged forward. "After I saw Sheriff Leavitt today, I couldn't stop thinking about the accident. I know I came to when he was bending over me. I'm sure of it."

"And that memory's what caused you to run off the road?"

"No, it wasn't that. It was..." She sighed and eased back, letting her hips rest against the sofa's sturdy back. She felt as if she needed to lean on something.

"When I started for home, I kept playing Leavitt's voice over and over in my head."

"What he said today?"

"What he said to me after the accident."

"When he told you to hold on, not to die."

"Yes, that's what he said to me. I was on the ground, and he was over me, and I knew I couldn't die, that there was something I had to tell him. Something important."

"What?"

She rubbed her forehead. An ache had started just behind her eyes. "I don't know. But before he was there, I remember..." She stopped, suddenly reluctant to call it all back.

But Reid didn't let her stop. "What? What do you remember?"

"That it was storming that night, a big storm, with wind and rain and thunder," she said, feeling as if she was reciting something she had written. She closed her eyes, seeing the bold streaks of light that had lit up the graveled drive that ran from the big house out to the road. She could hear the rumbles overhead, hear the rain beating on the roof of her mother's car. And she could see...

Shivering, she looked up at Reid, who was waiting, an expectant look on his face. "I remember..." she began again, then swallowed.

"What?"

"My mother."

"What was she doing?"

"Driving the car." Caroline blinked, trying to bring the scene into focus.

"Is that all?"

"She was screaming."

Reid reached out, took hold of her hand and held it tightly. Just like earlier today, at the library, his touch gave her strength.

"Why was she screaming?" he pressed.

"Grandfather..." Chills chased up Caroline's spine as she conjured up his face. "He was running alongside the car, trying to stop us."

"How?"

"The window was open. I don't know why. But rain was coming in, blowing in on Mother. Grandfather was reaching in, too, fighting her for the steering wheel."

"And she was screaming for him to stop?"

"No. She was screaming about Adam."

Reid frowned. "About your brother? What did she say?"

There was a hum inside Caroline's head. The same sound that had enveloped her out on the road just before she'd crashed into the ditch. It was like a wall, that sound. Like the wind and the rain on the night her mother died. With that sound in her head, it wasn't easy to concentrate or to remember. The sound blended everything together.

But by gripping her hands, Reid forced her to hold on to the memory. "What did your mother say?"

"'You stole my boy. You took my Adam.'"

"What?"

"She said it to Grandfather," Caroline murmured. "She kept screaming it over and over. 'You stole my boy. You took my Adam.'"

"And your grandfather?"

Frowning, concentrating with all her might, Caroline forced herself to see it all, feel it all. The rain. The lightning. The screaming fury of her mother's voice. The pounding of her own heart. The coppery taste of fear flooding her mouth. And her grandfather...

She could see him. Running, reaching....

"Bellowing," she whispered. "He was bellowing."

She sucked in her breath, staring up at Reid.

"Bellowing?" he repeated.

"Like a dragon."

The realization struck her like water hitting grease. It sputtered and sizzled inside her. "It's like my book," she told Reid. "Like the dragon in my book."

"What book?"

"The new one." She went to the desk, sorted through a sheaf of papers until she found the one she sought. It was the beginning of her new book, the passage she had written the night after running into Reid and Sammi for the first time in town. She thrust the paper into his hands. "Read it."

The scene was set in a boat on a storm-tossed sea. Mai, the character Reid remembered Caroline reading about earlier today, was being pursued across the water by a dragon. A dragon who bellowed fire in the rain.

"I've had a dream about that boat in a storm for years," Caroline said when he looked from the page to her. "But when I came back here, the dragon appeared, became part of it."

"And you wrote about it?"

"I've always written about my dreams," she explained. "I believe that's how I dealt with everything, especially with losing my twin brother."

"You turned him into a character."

"A character who is very real to me. As real as the dragon."

"Your grandfather." Since Reid's best memory of Robert Parrish was of a blustering man who regularly tried to devour their family farm, the characterization was appropriate.

Caroline was pacing the room, hands rubbing her arms as if she were chilled. "I understand it now. The boat in my dream is like my mother's car. And there's the rain. The storm." She stopped near the front door and put her hands to her mouth, drawing in another deep breath before adding, "And then there's the dragon."

"What did he say?" Reid asked her.

She turned, frowning. "What?"

"That night. You said your grandfather was bellowing. Was he saying something?"

Her brow furrowed. "I'm not...I can't..." She put her hands to her temples and pressed inward. "I can't remember."

"Maybe it doesn't matter."

"But it does. I'm sure it does." There was frustration in her voice. Reid could see the pain in her face.

"Stop trying so hard," he told her. "Maybe if you don't try—"

"But I've done that," she retorted. "Don't you understand? I spent years and years doing everything I could not to remember."

"Then you decided you had to know."

"Wouldn't you?"

He hesitated. "I'm not sure."

She raked her hands through her hair. "You're right. I'm not so sure, either. Lately, I've been thinking it might not be worth it. What happened that night might be so terrible, so awful, that I'll regret knowing." Her laughter had an edge to it, as if she was struggling for control. "I mean, look at today. I scared off poor old Sheriff Leavitt and then I ran my car into a ditch. If I remember everything, what's going to happen?"

"What's going to happen if you don't? Are you going to quietly go mad?"

His questions knocked her backward, as effectively as if he had struck her. She turned away and put her hands over her face.

Guilt clamping down on his gut like a vise, Reid crossed the room, took her hands, and pulled her into his arms. "I'm sorry." With his face pressed to her sweet-smelling hair, he repeated, "I'm sorry I said that."

Against his chest, she murmured, "It's not anything I haven't said to myself." She pulled away, tipped her face back to gaze up at him. "If I don't remember I probably will lose my mind." A half smile touched her lips. "That won't surprise you, will it?"

"I think that if you were going to go insane, it would have happened long before now."

"That's not what you used to think."

"Aren't I allowed to change my mind?"

She settled against him with a sigh, her arms slipping around him, holding on just as she had done earlier when he'd found her beside the road. "Hold me," she said, the entreaty as simple and direct as a child's. "I feel safe when you hold me, Reid. Safer than I've ever felt in my life."

He lifted his hand, touched her hair, something akin to wonder licking through him. "You shouldn't feel safe."

"Why?"

"Because I was the one who sent you back to the dragon." He remembered, quite clearly, the night he had delivered her home to Applewood. He saw Robert Parrish at the door. Stern. Unyielding. A cold light in his eyes. And yet Reid had turned away and left Caroline with him. What had the man done to her that she couldn't remember? The possibilities made his stomach churn.

She stirred against him now, but didn't look up. "I told you before that I don't blame you for taking me home."

"But if I hadn't brought you to him. If you had stayed with us—"

"Grandfather would never have allowed that. You would have just bought yourself more trouble than you could afford. I would have hated that."

"But you were so frightened. If we had called the authorities, got you some help—"

"They would have said the same thing you did. That I was a hysterical teenager."

"But maybe not."

Now she drew back, her dark eyes troubled. "Reid, you can't do this. You can't play what-if. I've tried it all my life. Maybe that's what made me into a writer.

But that's the only good that comes of guessing games. Otherwise, it's bad for you. It's frustrating. It just leaves you with this ache that never goes away."

Reid knew she was right. For he was aching from the might-have-beens that were spinning through his head. What might have happened if he had listened to her, believed in her all those years ago? Would she have avoided years of battling an unnameable terror? And what about his brother? What might have happened to Kevin if Reid hadn't sent Caroline away? That night had been a turning point. What might have been the result if he, Reid, had chosen the better path?

He couldn't answer those questions, couldn't bear torturing himself with the possible answers. Only one thing was for sure. Caroline had him pegged. All his life he had been so right. So certain of each and every step. Surprises had blocked his path—Kevin's leaving, Tonya's betrayal—but he had climbed over them, his eyes fixed straight ahead. Maybe if he had been a little less rigid, a little more willing to see things from another person's point of view...

But he couldn't change past mistakes. He could only control the future and avoid further calamities.

Like the blunder he was about to make. The mistake of keeping Caroline in his arms. Of lowering his mouth to hers.

He considered his options for maybe half a second.

Then he kissed her.

Caroline supposed she could have protested. She *should* have protested. With the weight of the emotional baggage she carried around with her, the last thing she needed to add to the load was this complication. She didn't need this big, disturbingly masculine man stirred into the mix. Sex was one of her failing points. And she didn't need to fail. Not now. Not when she could feel an avalanche of years of fear and panic beating down on her.

And yet she kissed him back.

Because she wanted it. Because it felt so damn good to want a man. To shiver from the pressure of his mouth moving against hers. To open her lips. To welcome the gentle invasion of his tongue. To feel his big hands roaming up her back, cupping her neck, spreading through her hair. To not be afraid or ashamed of the warm, liquid push of desire that spread downward through her body.

For all of her life, the touch of a man had shut down her senses.

The touch of this man set them free.

She broke the kiss and stepped back, cupping his face in her hands. "I want you," she said, words she had never spoken.

Reid caught her hand, drew it to his mouth. "I don't know if that's wise."

"But I need you. With you I can forget."

His eyebrows met in a frown. "Forget?"

"When you hold me, I forget to be afraid."

He studied her for a moment, then touched her face gently. "All right. Then let's forget."

Chapter Six

She expected to feel shy. But she didn't. She expected awkwardness. It didn't come. She trusted Reid so much. It felt natural to take his hand, to lead him into her bedroom.

Night had fallen. The open screen window above her bed let in the song of insects and the nightly serenade of frogs from down by the creek. Light from a utility pole just outside the house spread in a buttery arc, bleeding through sheer curtains that billowed in a warm, dying breeze.

And Caroline's nerves, absent only a minute ago, sprang to life.

"It's warm in here," she said, and made a move toward the electric fan that stood on the bedside table.

Reid drew her back. "Don't. It's not that warm. And I'd rather listen to the sounds from outside." He brought her close, one hand on the small of her back, the other covering hers. He spoke close to her ear. "If we're really quiet, we might hear the train whistle from the other side of the ridge. There's one that rolls through most every night at this time. Just listen."

Caroline did, remembering when she used to sit on the front porch of the big house and do this very thing, straining for the faint sound of a whistle on the still evening air. But this time, instead of the train, all she could hear was the steady drumming of Reid's heart. Or was it her own? He was so close, she couldn't tell.

"Rain's coming," he murmured, his breath warm against her cheek. "Can you smell it?"

There was moisture in the air. But the only scent that mattered to Caroline was his—a mixture of earth and soap and male musk. She breathed it in, captured it just as his mouth closed once more on hers.

They swayed with the kiss, moving together in a rhythm that seemed to match the sounds of the night. As the kiss deepened, Reid lifted her up, the powerful muscles of his shoulders cording and bunching beneath her hands. And yet it seemed to require so little effort for him to pick her up, to set both of them down on the edge of the bed, where he held her across his lap, still kissing her.

Intoxicated by that kiss, she wanted it to go on and on. It was the sort of kiss she had dreamed about when she was a young girl who escaped whenever possible into the books and movies where a woman's heart could be won by a man's strong and sure and oh-so-right kiss. All these years she had heard about women who lost their heads with the right kiss from the right man. But gradually her girlhood dreams had faded under disappointing reality. Twelve years of marriage hadn't shown her the simple power of the right kiss. But now, with a man she had never dreamed of kissing, she knew the truth. She would never again doubt that bones could melt, limbs turn to jelly, or heads swim. Every cliché that had ever been applied to kisses came true for her in Reid's arms.

When he pulled away, she whimpered a protest. But that quickly turned to a sigh of pleasure as his lips strayed from her jaw to her neck and then back to her mouth.

"You taste sweet," he murmured between light, nibbling kisses. "Sweet and soft." One hand slipped from the back of her neck to her hair, his fingers threading through the strands, coaxing her head back so that her mouth tilted upward, opening, blooming beneath his kiss.

She turned toward him, toward the kiss, while the hand that was pressed against his body worked with the buttons on his shirt. Three buttons were quickly undone, and she slipped her hand inside, her fingers splaying wide on the warm skin of his chest. Her fingertips brushed through light whorls of hair and feathered downward, skimming across a flat nipple that tightened with her touch.

He broke away from the kiss and drew in a sharp breath, his hand closing over hers, briefly holding her fingers on that small, cresting bit of flesh. Caroline could feel the shock of pleasure that went through his body. Amazed by that strong reaction, she circled his nipple with her thumb. Once, twice. And again. Reid leaned back, chin lifting, as he groaned her name. His response intrigued her. She had never explored a man's body enough to know a touch like this would bring such pleasure.

Made bold by that knowledge, heady with the power she had to make him respond, she pushed his shirt further apart and dipped her head forward, letting her tongue take over the strokes of her thumb.

Reid leaned back, arms braced behind him. Caroline shifted, too, half kneeling on the bed beside him, one foot on the floor, hands working his shirt free of his pants, undoing the rest of the buttons, while her lips teased one nipple and then the other. When his shirt was open and his body felt as tense as a tightly strung bow beneath her touch, he moved again, pulling her across him, so that when he sat up, she was on her knees, straddling his hips.

His lips again slanted across hers, coaxing a guttural cry she barely recognized as her own. He pushed his hands up her thighs and beneath the full skirt that had bunched between their bodies. Round and round his palms massaged her legs, slowly caressing her skin, his fingers hard and yet so gentle, building a fire in the pit of her belly.

Against her mouth, he murmured, "Get up, sweetheart." She obeyed like a woman in a stupor, straightening, her knees pressing into the mattress. Before she could adequately follow his intent, he had pulled the front buttons of her skirt apart and was tossing the colorful garment aside. Because it had been so warm today, she hadn't bothered with a slip or panty hose, and all that covered her mound from his gaze or his touch was a pair of plain, white cotton panties.

Caroline struggled with shyness and nerves that tried to edge past the excitement uncurling inside her. "I don't wear silk," she whispered, settling her hands on Reid's shoulders.

"I don't care." He looked up at her. His gaze locked with hers, though his hands were once more slipping up her thighs. "I don't give a damn about silk or satin."

One of his fingertips teased the elastic edge of her panties, and she caught her breath. Her legs felt trembly and weak. She started to edge downward, but Reid's strong hands held her steady.

"Don't move, sweetheart," he crooned, still looking up and into her face. "Don't move." Once more, his thumb threaded beneath the thin cotton, moved inward, slowly, steadily, finally dipping into the moist cleft between her legs.

This time, she would have fallen if Reid's other hand hadn't been holding her up, if she hadn't braced her hands on his shoulders. But she didn't fall. She stayed where she was, accepting, *aching* for the next stroke of his fingers. He obliged, his thumb slipping inside the slick folds of her body, seeking and finding the delicate kernel of flesh that made her tremble even harder.

All her life, Caroline had shut down when a man touched her. Some voice inside her had commanded her not to feel, not to respond, not to lose control. She wasn't supposed to take pleasure this way. She was supposed to feel guilty if she did. Tonight was no exception. Even as moisture seeped from her, preparing her body to accept a man's entry, guilt and fear were thrumming through the darkness, waiting to swallow her, to rob her of the pleasure that waited just beyond the stroke of a man's thumb. She felt herself stiffen, begin to close up, close down. She began pushing away from Reid, trying to draw her legs together.

But he would have none of it. His thumb remained where it was, tempting, teasing, stroking. "Don't resist it," he told her. "Just open up, sweetheart. Open up for me."

Caroline closed her eyes and tried to block out everything but Reid's touch. But she didn't want to. She didn't want to lose control. For so long, it had been important not to lose herself in pleasure.

Her grandfather had told her that. She could remember him saying, *"You can't be like your mother. You can't lay down with just anyone. Your mother did. She ruined her life, ruined our name."*

Eyes flying open, Caroline gasped. What was she remembering? When did her grandfather say that to her?

"Caroline?" Reid murmured, his hands stilling as he looked up at her. "Are you okay? Did I hurt you?"

"No. No, of course not." She closed her eyes again. She shut out the voice in her head. She had carried that cautionary voice with her for so long, too long. But never, until now, had she heard those distinct words or known exactly whose voice she was hearing.

It belonged to the dragon.

Anger replaced the fear and the familiar rush of shame that had threatened to paralyze her. Why should the dragon control her now, even from his grave?

With Reid beside her, she could outrun the dragon, couldn't she?

Drawing in a deep breath, she looked down at Reid again. "Touch me," she told him. "Touch me again."

He did. And once more, excitement scorched through her. Liquid warmth beaded in her most feminine depths. Once more her body began to open. Her senses began to soar.

She could feel the dragon's breath on her heels.

But she was faster. Reid was stronger. And he carried her over the edge, into a freefall of sensation.

The dragon was gone.

More important, he was wrong.

Reid felt Caroline's climax rip through her body. Sweetly powerful. Intoxicating. While she trembled, he carried her back on the bed with him, catching her soft cries of completion beneath his kiss.

"I want you," she told him, much as she had done before. "I want you now."

He was hard for her. His sex was heavy, distended to the point of pain as he shed his pants and briefs. Her panties were slipped off and away, and yet as he knelt between her thighs, he hesitated. "It's been a long time for me, Caroline."

She touched the side of his face and gently combed back his hair. "For me, too."

"I want it to be right."

"But it already is."

"Caroline . . ."

"Shh." Reaching down between their bodies, she took him into her hand, her fingers enfolding his heat, stoking a fire that didn't need tending. He jerked under her touch, and though he didn't believe it was possible, he grew even harder.

"You shouldn't do that," he warned, though he didn't want her to stop.

"Then what about this." Tilting her pelvis upward, she guided him into her body.

A cry tore from his throat as he sank into her. A cry to match the rising joy of his senses. She was tight and warm and fit him so well. Too well, he feared, as his first glide into her welcoming body threatened to bring him completion. But he held on. And she wound herself around him, sinuous as a cat. They found a rhythm. She lifted her hips, meeting his thrusts, purring when he withdrew. She was soft. She was firm. She was a silky ride up a vast height.

But most of all, she was just Caroline. She was fragile and strong. Complex enough to confound him. Intriguing enough to have led him here. To her bed. Into this dark, secret communion of body and spirit.

He spilled into her with a groan, eager for the thrill yet sorry to feel it ending. Like a kid on a roller coaster heading for the final curve, he leaned back, held back, trying to stretch it out, make it last. But Caroline whispered his name and he was lost. She pulled him forward, into a wrenching burst of pleasure.

His only regret was that he knew she didn't follow him in that last rush of speed.

For a moment Reid let his weight rest on her. But he was heavy, his body as drenched with perspiration as hers. He slipped to her side and they lay, still in the sultry night air, listening to the world just outside the window, a world they had forgotten existed.

For just a little longer he wanted that world to stay away.

When his breathing returned to normal, he lifted his head and looked at Caroline. Her face was turned away from him. But the light from outside revealed the rest of her. She lay in an elegant sprawl of limbs, still wearing the white ruffled blouse that was now hiked up under her breasts. One hand rested on her belly. The other was flung outward. One knee was drawn up. The other, closest to him, was straight. And between her thighs was a dusky, midnight shadow.

That was where he touched her. He placed his hand over her heat.

She looked at him, and he turned on his side, curving his body around hers. He rested his chin on her shoulder and smiled. "You okay?"

"Better than that."

"But you didn't—"

"I didn't have to."

"I wanted you to."

With slow, circular motions, he massaged her midnight-shadowed mound. She sighed and pulled one knee even further back. His fingers slipped downward. He saw her eyes widen, felt her indrawn breath.

"Reid?"

"Shh," he said, pressing a kiss to her shoulder. "Just go with it, okay?"

Her hips rocked upward, meeting his touch. He kept stroking, his gaze never wavering from her face, until a cry spilled out of her and her body trembled, until she caught his hand with her own and made him stop.

Then she turned into his arms again, almost sobbing his name.

"Next time," he murmured against her lips. "Next time you'll feel like that when I'm inside of you. Next time. I promise."

They fell asleep that way. Wrapped together despite the heat.

And sometime later, when the rain had begun, he made good on his promise.

Reid left about three in the morning. Caroline didn't want him to go, but she didn't try to make him stay. He had a farm to run. The morning milking would start at sunrise. His daughter would be home soon after that. Life couldn't stop because of what had transpired between them tonight.

So they kissed goodbye on the front steps. He promised to call her later. She stood, wrapped in her faded terry-cloth robe, and watched him drive away. When he was gone, she sat down on the old porch rocker. The rain had ended nearly as quickly as it had begun, and already the moon was peeping out from the clouds. There was no way she would be able to go back to sleep.

She wondered, when the reality of what had happened settled in on him, if Reid would regret tonight. Or would she?

Sighing, she set the rocker in motion. She replayed each touch, each flutter of excitement she had known in his arms. Flushing, she remembered being bold, so much bolder than she had ever dreamed possible. She remembered pleasuring him and accepting pleasure. In so many different ways.

Tonight, she had beaten the dragon.

But she didn't want to think about that. She didn't want memories of her grandfather to intrude on what she was feeling inside. Most of all, she didn't want to remember anything more of the night her mother died. She was tired of trying. She had turned to Reid tonight to forget. And she had. With him, she had conquered a fear, a barrier that had stood in her way all of her adult life. Maybe that was enough.

Buoyed by that thought, she went inside. She needed to write. Tonight, while she was feeling on top of the world, she would find a way for the princess in her book to thwart her own dragons. With that in mind, she returned to a passage she had worked on just after coming home to Applewood, to the villain who, against her wishes, had taken on Reid's face.

Now, instead of a villain, she made him a hero. A knight who could pull the stars down from the sky, who rode through the heavens on a great, winged bird. She named him Roark, a man strong enough to fight for his honor, tender enough to tug at a princess's heart.

She plotted and planned, weaving her new hero into the story she had already outlined. By morning, when Caroline flipped off her computer and went to bed, the only question she couldn't answer was whether the interest that sparked between the princess and her knight would flower into something more than mere passion.

It was the same question she asked about Reid and herself as morning blended to afternoon and evening, and he didn't call.

Caroline wanted to call him, but wasn't sure if she should. She had never had a lover before. A husband, yes. But that had been different. She and Harry had come together out of need and fear and loneliness. They had moved in with one another first, because neither of them could afford rent on a decent place on their own. They married because Harry thought she would respond to him in bed if she had a marriage license. She had gone along with him because she did want that license, that security, and she had wanted to respond. She had yearned for children they never had. For a closeness they never felt. She had tried to be the wife he needed and deserved. But he had never been the right man.

Was Reid?

By seven o'clock that night, Caroline knew she had a couple of choices. She could sit here, hoping he would call. Or she could take matters into her own hands and go after him. Before this summer, she probably would have waited. But not now. Now she knew how to go after what she wanted.

So she drove over to Reid's.

Sammi answered the doorbell. Her blue eyes widened in surprise, followed by a satisfied smile. "Come on in."

Caroline followed her into the front foyer and handed over a book. "I thought you might want an advance copy of the *Seers* book that'll be in the stores this fall." The book, which had arrived from her editor in the afternoon mail, had provided Caroline with a convenient excuse.

"You're kidding," Sammi said. "I get to read it before anyone else?" She let out a squeal of excitement, leaping forward to give Caroline a hug, a move that rattled the china figurines in the cabinet beneath the stairs.

"Sammi, what in—"

Reid's hastily ended question made Caroline turn around. He stood in a doorway that, if she remembered correctly, led to the kitchen. He had a skillet in one hand, a dish towel in the other, and he was scowling at her.

His daughter went to him, waving the book and explaining. But Reid just looked at Caroline.

He had thought about calling her all day. He had gone so far as to plan the speech he was going to make. All about how they had been foolish and impulsive. How he had gotten caught up in the emotion of her fight to recover her memories. How they had made a mistake.

But he hadn't called. For one thing, he was afraid hearing her voice would render him speechless. And for another, he knew his reasoning was fatally flawed. Perhaps making wild, mindless love *once* could be chalked up to impulse. But the kind of love they had made had required thought. It had been wild, but there had been plenty of moments when he might have stopped. And it hadn't been just once. There had been that second time, when he had lifted her onto his body, had stripped away her blouse and bra, had pressed his lips to each of her small, pebbling breasts, and—

"Dad!"

"What?" he snapped at his daughter, then was instantly contrite. He took a deep breath, trying to clear the wanton image of making love to Caroline from his brain. He focused on Sammi. "I'm sorry, Cookie. I wasn't listening."

"Obviously." She darted a look between him and Caroline.

Caroline stepped forward. She looked a little flushed, leading Reid to think she had been following the direction of his thoughts. It wasn't the first time he had suspected her of mind-reading. "I brought this over to Sammi," she said, pointing to the book the girl held up. "And I wanted to talk to you, too."

"I'm doing the dishes." The excuse was feeble, but he didn't care.

"I'll do them," Sammi said, taking the skillet and the towel out of his hands.

Of all the times for his daughter to volunteer for the "grunge work," as she called it, this wasn't the one Reid would have chosen. But to refuse would only put off the inevitable and make Sammi ask too many questions.

"I have some work I have to do down at the machine shed," he told Caroline. "We can talk there."

"But Dad—" Sammi protested.

"What now?"

"The machine shed?"

"Yes. I have something to do that can't wait. I'm sure Caroline understands." His actual goal was to get

Caroline away from the house and his daughter's habit of nosing into business that didn't concern her.

"All right," the teenager conceded, but she didn't look any too happy about it.

Reid preceded Caroline out the back way, through the kitchen and across the screened back porch. When they were clear of the house and moving past the bed of shoulder-high dahlias that grew near the edge of the yard, Caroline said, "I think Sammi's on to us."

Reid turned to look at her, prepared to say that henceforth there would nothing for Sammi to be "on to" them about. But he didn't get the words out. Instead he blurted out the first thing that came to mind. "You look beautiful."

Caroline blinked. "What?"

He cleared his throat, aggravated at himself, though he had only spoken the truth. The vividly colored flowers bloomed around her, the perfect foil for her honeyed skin and black hair, while the fading summer sunlight bathed her in gold. But the way she looked went deeper than the superficial. There was a new softness about her, a tenderness that touched her eyes as she looked at him. Damn, but she was hard to resist. She would be difficult to forget.

"Reid?" she said.

But instead of repeating that she was beautiful, he just reached out and took her hand.

Smiling slightly, she twined her fingers through his. "I was afraid you were angry or something."

Still holding her hand, he set off again, but he didn't look at her. "Not angry, no."

"But you didn't..."

She didn't allow herself to complete the sentence, but Reid could fill in the blank. He hadn't called, after he said he would. "It was a busy day," he lied. He felt the disbelieving look she sent his way, but he didn't say anything more.

He hadn't really been lying about needing to work down here. His tractor was still a mess. A fact that gave him a guilty nudge as he ushered Caroline inside the cement block machine shed and garage. He turned on the bare light bulb that swung from the high ceiling and looked at the offending piece of machinery in disgust. If his mind had been on his business instead of Caroline, he might have made some progress today. He couldn't afford more days like today, and he positively couldn't afford this woman.

She stopped just shy of the parts and tools that were fanned out on the uneven concrete floor around the tractor. "This looks pretty serious."

"It is."

"What's wrong?"

Easing down on a old stool at his worktable, Reid sighed and snapped on the set of shop lights that hung overhead. He was tired, had been tired all day, a fact that proved he was well past the age when he could make love all night and then try to work the next day. Before Caroline showed up, he had been planning to get the dishes out of the way and go straight to bed.

He studied the woman standing in front of him for a moment, wondering why she didn't look as exhausted as he felt. In her crisp, white cotton shorts and red knit top, she looked as fresh as morning. But then, she had probably spent the day resting while he had been out trying his damnedest to make a living. Their lives were worlds apart. Too far apart for what had happened last night to have meaning beyond the sensations of the moment.

"Come on, Caroline," he said, an edge to his voice. "We both know we didn't come out here to discuss my bad luck with farming equipment."

"No, I guess we didn't."

Silence reigned again until he asked, "Well? Who's going to start?"

She laughed, a high, nervous sound. "Why is it that you don't seem quite like the man who drove away from my place this morning?"

"'Cause I guess I'm not that man."

"Oh? Then who was he?"

"A damn fool."

She bit her lower lip and simply looked at him, her eyes full of hurt.

He couldn't take that look. He had to avoid it if he wanted to get this over with. Glancing down, he plucked a screwdriver from among the tools on the worktable. He turned it over and over in his hands as he started the speech he had prepared earlier today. "Last night shouldn't have happened, Caroline."

"But it did. I wanted it to."

"It was a mistake. You were upset. I was feeling..." He swallowed, fumbling for the right words. "I was feeling—"

"Hot?"

Caroline's suggestion brought his head up. Anger had replaced the hurt in her expression.

"Hot, horny, randy," she continued. "Aren't those the words that describe how you felt?"

"No," he told her, feeling a jab of anger himself. "Those aren't the right words. I didn't come to your little program at the library with the intention of taking you home to bed. That certainly wasn't what was on my mind after I found you and your car in a ditch."

"Then you deny being attracted to me before last night?"

"No...I mean, yes."

"If you weren't attracted to me, why did you kiss me the other day down at the creek?"

"That was just—"

"Another mistake?"

"Yes."

She lifted an eyebrow. "My, my, but you seem to be making lots of mistakes these days, Mr. McClure. That's not like you."

"I've been doing a lot of foolish things since you came back here."

"But last night wasn't one of them."

"Yes, it was," he insisted, and glanced down at the tool he held in a white-knuckled grip. Somehow he had to get the words out, get them right, and send her on her way. "Last night, you needed someone, and I just happened to be there. It wasn't special. It certainly wasn't the start of—"

He never finished the sentence. For something flew through the air just past his head and banged up against the cement block wall. He lunged off his stool and gaped at Caroline, who stood with her arm cocked back to throw something else.

He swore at her. "What are you doing?"

"You're not getting away with this," she told him. "You're not going to tell me that last night wasn't special or meaningful to you. I may not be the most experienced woman in the world, but you can't tell me that what happened between us was just your everyday, ordinary, garden variety sex."

"I didn't say—"

"Yes, you did." She launched another missile at him, her aim just as bad this time. But this one hit the shop light over the table, bounced to the floor, and then came perilously close to his head.

"Caroline!" Reid yelled. "What are you trying to do, take me out?" Halfway expecting another attack, he crouched down. At his feet lay her weapon, a wrench. He shook it at her. "This could have killed me."

In answer, she burst out in laughter.

Standing, he glared at her, protesting, "It isn't funny."

But all Caroline could do was laugh.

Finally, Reid just joined in. It was either that or throw the damn wrench back at her.

A few moments later, wiping tears of laughter from her cheeks, Caroline said, "I wish you could have seen your face. You came off of that stool like a rocket."

"You scared the hell out of me," he retorted, sitting back down on the stool.

"I've never done anything like that before in my life. I can't ever remember trying to hit anyone, even as a kid."

"Obviously. Your aim was damn bad."

Chin lifting, she said, "I'll get it right next time." She knelt down and hefted another weapon, this time a vital part from the tractor.

He raised his hands in surrender. "Don't, Caroline, please."

"Then stop lying to me." Quickly as it had appeared, her laughter was gone, replaced by a deadly serious expression. They were back where they had started.

But Reid wasn't ready to give in. "I'm not lying, Caroline. Last night—"

"Was pretty damn wonderful."

He couldn't look her in the eyes and lie yet again. He knew the best thing for them both might be to hurt her so badly that she turned and walked out of here without a backward glance. He should tell her that last night was nothing but sex, that she would just someone he had used to slake his lust. But he couldn't do it.

"All right," he admitted. "Last night was...special."

She lowered her arm, dropped the tractor part to the floor and walked toward him. "So what do we do about it?"

"Do?"

"Do we just let something special and wonderful go?"

He took a deep breath. "You and I don't belong together, Caroline."

She stopped in front of him. Close. Far too close for him to maintain any indifference. "How do you know we don't belong together?" she asked.

Crossing his arms, Reid avoided her eyes. He didn't want to be trapped by that wide, ebony gaze. He had to keep his distance, physical and mental. He had to force the images from last night out of his mind. He had to forget the scent of her perfume, the feel of her body moving against his, and the sound she had made when she climaxed. He had to stop thinking with his sex. That wasn't easy, since his body had decided to take a distinctly hard approach to her proximity.

But he made himself frown at her. "I would think you'd know the reasons we don't belong together by heart by now."

He was talking about Kevin, Caroline thought. Even after last night, he still blamed her for the loss of his brother. She shouldn't be surprised. Hadn't he said just the day before yesterday that Kevin was a subject they should avoid? One night of passion wasn't about to erase years of bitterness.

But she couldn't let him go. She couldn't let this man just force her out of his life. His touch warmed her in a way that no other's ever had. Having discovered that she could burn for a man, she didn't want to douse the flame. If what they had together went up in smoke, then so be it. But they owed it to themselves to find out for sure.

Her desire to know made her brave. Before last night she could never have challenged the ferocious frown on his face to reach out and touch his cheek. She could never have stepped closer. She could never have put her hand on his knee and forced him to look into her eyes. But she could do all those things now. And she did.

"I want you to tell me to go," she told him, holding his gaze steady with her own. "If you can do that, I'll walk out and not come back."

"All right, go."

She stroked her hand up his thigh. "You have to mean it."

She saw the muscles working in his throat as her fingers neared his crotch. "I mean it," he whispered.

Her fingers skimmed away from their mark, but teased their way back slowly. "You don't."

Now there was a challenge in his gaze, an I-dare-you tilt to his chin. "Go, Caroline."

Where he wanted her to go had nothing to do with leaving. And she wanted to prove to him and to herself that she could play this teasing game out to the end. But she was new to flirtation, new to temptation, and at the last minute her courage deserted her. She couldn't place her hand over his crotch.

"Looks like I win," he said.

She dropped her gaze to his lap, to what looked like a distinct bulge. "No," she said, looking up at him again. "Looks like I'm the winner."

And then she cupped him with her hand.

That ridge beneath his soft, faded jeans stirred against her palm.

Pulling her between his widespread legs, Reid sighed in defeat, although he couldn't stop the smile that tugged at his mouth. "I was betrayed."

"And you enjoyed it." Smiling, she lifted her lips to his.

He had lost his mind, Reid decided as they kissed. Lost it to a raven-haired witch whose best spell was wide-eyed innocence. A Parrish witch, who seemed to greet every new bit of sexual play with wonder and discovery. It didn't say much for the man she had been married to for twelve years. Or maybe it said a whole lot for the strength of the pull between them.

Reid knew he should fight it. Trouble was, he couldn't think about that with her in his arms.

As soon as he gave in, the kiss went completely out of control. His shirt got unbuttoned. Her blouse came halfway off. Reid had lifted her to the edge of his worktable and was considering the erotic possibilities or impossibilities of that position when he heard the door open behind him.

Thinking of Sammi, he turned, shielding Caroline.

And found young Mr. Kirk Williams standing in the doorway.

Chapter Seven

If Caroline weren't so embarrassed, she might have felt sorry for the young people who were seated across the kitchen from the cabinets where she stood. But she was too rattled to care too much about Sammi and Kirk's fate. Although it could have been worse. Kirk might have opened the shed door ten minutes later, and she and Reid could have been caught in an even more compromising position. Since Sammi had arrived on the scene right after Kirk, they had narrowly avoided major humiliation.

Caroline wanted to kick herself for being so careless.

Reid probably did, too. But most of all, he was furious that Sammi had been sneaking out to meet Kirk again. Caroline was frankly surprised that the girl would take such a chance and try to meet Kirk right under Reid's nose before it was completely dark outside. As Sammi had explained it, Reid had been talking about going to bed early all during dinner. Pretending to call her best friend, she had alerted Kirk and invited him over. Caroline's appearance spoiled her plans, and Sammi hadn't been able to reach Kirk by phone to warn him away. Then he had parked over on the old logging road by the creek and shown up early.

And had been caught. Or had done the catching. Caroline wasn't sure which was more appropriate.

On the other side of the kitchen, Reid hung up the telephone. White lines framed his mouth as he turned toward the two teenagers. "Your father said for you to get home *now,*" he told Kirk. "And he knows you're not to come back."

Chair legs scraped across the floor as Kirk pushed away from the table. His shoulders were straight and his blond head held high as he sauntered toward the back door. He even had the moxie to look over his shoulder and say, "I'll see you soon, Sammi."

Reid struck like a snake, coming across the room before anyone could react. "You little smart—"

Caroline threw herself between him and Kirk, while Sammi screamed his name and came around the table.

"Don't hit him," Caroline told Reid. "You'll never forgive yourself if you hit him."

Her words must have struck home, because Reid let her push him away. Kirk flattened himself to the wall beside the door, his chest heaving and eyes darting toward Sammi, who had stopped in the middle of the kitchen.

She demanded of Reid, "Why are you trying to ruin my life this way?"

"You're doing this to yourself," her father shot back. "You're the one who invited him over here."

Sammi tried to form a protest, but Reid cut her off.

"I don't know what's wrong with you these days, Sammi. You don't seem to hear me when I tell you what's what."

"But you don't—"

"But nothing." Reid's gaze whipped back toward the boy. "Didn't you know that Sammi wasn't supposed to see you?"

Kirk's answer was a cocked eyebrow.

"Then what were you doing here?" Reid demanded. It was a question he had already asked, with the same results he was getting now, but Caroline supposed he had to keep pressing.

Straightening away from the wall, Kirk regained some of his poise and looked Reid straight in the eye for the first time this evening. "Maybe I think Sammi's worth the risk," he said. There was nothing smart in the words or his tone. There was simple honesty in his gaze.

Caroline had to give him points for that. In fact, she didn't think Kirk was living up to the punk label Reid had placed on him. Earlier, when he had surprised them down at the shed, he could have just run away. In her book, a punk would have run. But he hadn't left Sammi to face the music on her own, and he hadn't tried to lie his way out of the jam. That told Caroline there was something more to this boy than his reputation. Perhaps that something was why he held such fascination for a girl as bright as Sammi.

But Reid quite obviously didn't care. "I want you out of here," he told Kirk. "I told your father—"

"I don't know why you had to call him," the boy retorted. "I haven't done anything wrong." Once more his gaze skipped to Sammi. "*We* haven't done anything wrong."

"Let's make sure that stays that way." Reid jabbed his finger in the air to punctuate his warning. "*You* stay away from my daughter. Stay off my property, out of my shed."

"Planning on using it with your girlfriend yourself?" Kirk flung at him.

Caroline had to dig in her heels to maintain a grip on Reid, who started toward him again. "Just leave," she told Kirk. "Go. Now."

He did. But not without one final look at Sammi. Caroline guessed this wasn't the last that would be heard from Kirk Williams. She didn't let go of Reid until the screen door on the back porch slammed shut.

But there was still Sammi to face. Cheeks red, hands clenched at her side, she said, "You're such a hypocrite, Dad."

"Go to your room" was his tight reply.

"So you and Caroline can be alone?" she taunted.

"Even if that's what we wanted, it would be none of your business."

"But me and Kirk, that's *your* business?"

It was typical teenage logic, but instead of insisting she go and cool down, Reid retorted, "When you're an adult—"

"Something I can't wait for," the girl cut in. "I can't wait to get out of here and get away from you. Because I hate you. I hate you so much!"

Caroline saw the pain that deepened the tired lines on Reid's face. She knew he was hearing those words and thinking of one thing—his brother. She thought of Kevin, too, of another summer night in this kitchen, when another angry young person had hit Reid with harsh, condemning words.

For a long moment Reid said nothing. Then he turned away from her, his face a dull red as he gripped the edge of the counter. "Get to bed, Sammi. Right now."

But his daughter was intent on pushing her luck. "That's right, send me to bed like a naughty little girl. You'd like it if I didn't grow up, wouldn't you? You'd like to run my life forever."

Reid said nothing, but the muscles in his jaw were clenched, his eyes were squeezed shut, as if he couldn't bear to hear any more.

This wasn't her family or her fight, but Caroline couldn't stand seeing his pain. "Sammi," she said, moving toward her with outstretched hands. "Go on up. Don't fight about it anymore."

"So you're on his side now?" the girl demanded.

"This isn't about sides."

The tears Sammi had held in for the past half hour now overflowed as she confronted Caroline. "You're the one who said all he wanted to do was control people. And you're the one who told me you had to sneak out and meet Uncle Kevin down at the shed."

Reid jerked around and looked at Caroline. "You told her that?"

"Before I knew how you felt about Kirk."

"Damn it, Caroline—"

"What's the matter, Dad?" Sammi said with a sneer. "Are you upset to find out the shed is where she used to go with Uncle Kevin, too?"

The cruelness of that jibe took Caroline's breath.

It almost knocked Reid to the floor.

And the minute she said it, he saw the regret that filled his daughter's eyes. It was so like her, to lash out that way, trying to cover all her feelings with anger. He knew, because it was his way, as well.

Her breath caught on a sob. "Oh, Dad...Daddy, I'm sorry. Caroline, I didn't mean..."

Feeling a million years old, he rubbed his hand across his eyes. "Go on, Sammi. Just go on up to bed."

She turned and dashed away, her footsteps pounding up the front stairs, leaving him alone with Caroline.

He looked at the floor instead of at her. "I think maybe you should go, too."

"Reid..." She reached out and touched his arm. "Reid, I haven't encouraged Sammi with Kirk."

"I know that."

"But I'm sorry I interfered here, sorry I said anything."

"I'm sure you were only trying to help."

"But I didn't."

"Please." He looked up and into her dark, concerned eyes. "Could you please just go?"

"But I want—"

"To do what?" he snapped, shaking her hand off his arm. "There isn't anything I need or want you to do."

In the silence that followed, the clock on the windowsill ticked, the refrigerator hummed and Caroline continued to stand, her gaze steady on his.

"Please go," he repeated.

"All right," she said, turning toward the door. "I'll talk to you tomorrow."

"No. You won't. Just stay away, Caroline."

Her step faltered. Scarlet stained her cheeks. But she said nothing, and she left.

Thank God she left.

Reid didn't know if he could have argued with her if she had insisted on staying. He was so tired that the room was spinning in front of his eyes. He felt every day of his forty-five years and then some. Slowly he went through the house, turning out lights and creeping upstairs.

Exhaustion claimed him almost instantly. But he dreamed about Kevin, about welcoming him home. Except when he went to hug him, Kevin turned to dust. Reid was left holding a cloud that disappeared. Profoundly disturbed, Reid awakened and lay in the darkness, feeling that dust on his hands.

He couldn't sleep after that. It was nearly four, and he usually rose at five, anyway, so he got up. He went downstairs, brewed a pot of coffee and sat in the predawn quiet.

He couldn't stop thinking about what Sammi had said about Kevin and Caroline meeting down at the shed. Had they been lovers there? His brother had said no. And remembering the vehemence of that denial,

Reid was still inclined to accept it. He was silly to think about it, to feel so guilty, as if he was betraying Kevin.

Caroline was the one who had let Kevin down. Years ago. When she filled him full of nonsense and then left him here without a backward glance. Without Caroline's influence, Kevin wouldn't be dust in the ground.

Even as he repeated that familiar accusation to himself, Reid let the doubts creep in. Caroline said she went away because she thought it was best for Kevin. She wanted to save him, she said, from all her problems. In that sense, she had wanted the same thing for his brother that Reid had wanted. And in point of fact, wasn't it Reid's fault that she had run away in the first place? If he hadn't taken her back to her grandfather...

Reid swore, forcing the doubts aside. But one by one, all the assumptions he had made about her were being challenged.

But that shouldn't matter. Even if he didn't take into account what had happened to Kevin because of her, Caroline wasn't a woman Reid should be wasting his time on. Not two days ago, he had told himself to find someone uncomplicated. Someone who wanted sex and an occasional night at the movies. Someone nice and simple and undemanding. But Caroline wanted more, needed more, would demand more than he had ever thought of giving.

She was as complex as they came. She had dragons in her past. And despite his natural protective instincts, he didn't want to be her knight.

Did he?

If that were true, why was it that he couldn't get the scent of her out of his nostrils, the feel of her off his hands, the taste of her out of his mouth?

Groaning, he buried his face in his hands.

When he looked up, Sammi stood on the other side of the table, a ghostly figure in her oversized white sleep shirt.

"You're up early," she said.

Reid picked up his coffee mug. "I couldn't sleep."

"Me, neither." She eased into the chair opposite his. The only light came from the lamp he had left on in the foyer behind her. It was too dark to read her expression, but he could feel her hesitation. "I'm sorry about what I said last night," she managed finally. "About Caroline and Uncle Kevin, that is."

He sighed. "It's okay, Cookie. We were all pretty upset."

"But I like Caroline. I like you with Caroline."

"I'm not *with* her."

"But you could be, couldn't you?"

He peered through the shadows at her, but made no reply.

"Just because she used to go out with Uncle Kevin, that wouldn't really stop you from seeing her, would it? No matter what I said last night."

In answer, Reid said, "Last night wasn't about me and Caroline."

"But Kirk said you and she were—"

"I kissed her," Reid cut in. He felt his face grow warm and was glad of the cover of darkness to hide it from his daughter's sharp-eyed gaze. "No matter what your punk boyfriend says, it was just a kiss." That was a lie, but he didn't care.

"You wouldn't call it *just* a kiss if it had been me and Kirk that you had walked in on."

The mere thought fisted Reid's hands. "Comparing you and Kirk Williams to me and Caroline isn't an argument that's going to get you anywhere. It didn't last night. It won't this morning."

"I just wish—"

"I'm not talking about this again, Sammi. You're fifteen—"

"Sixteen in fifty-two days."

The reminder was so familiar, he almost smiled. Every summer since she was a little girl she had counted down the days to her birthday, which fell on the last day of August. But she wasn't a little girl. Just as she had said last night, he couldn't send her up to her room and expect that she would emerge willing to obey him without argument.

Soon, she would walk out the front door. Just as Kevin had. Reid's throat tightened. No, she wouldn't be like Kevin. He couldn't let that happen.

Right now, she was still his responsibility. His alone. He had never felt the burden so acutely. He had never felt so alone.

And unaccountably, it was Caroline he yearned for.

Shaking off the thought, he looked at his daughter again. "I think it would be for the best if you and I didn't discuss Kirk again."

"But, Daddy, I want to talk about him."

Her manner of address as much as the pleading tone of her voice made Reid lean forward. "Why?"

"Because..." She hesitated.

He reached out and took hold of her hand, momentary panic churning through his gut. She wasn't a little girl anymore, but she was a long way from being ready for the kind of relationship he imagined a boy like Kirk Williams might want. "Is there something you need to tell me about you and this boy? Have you...he...has he done something you need to talk about?"

She pulled back. "Of course not. I'm not stupid, you know."

"Stupid doesn't have anything to do with it, Sammi. That boy—"

"You don't even know him."

"I know enough."

"But what about what I know? Aren't I smart enough to choose the right people as friends? What have I done that makes you distrust me?"

Reid responded with a short laugh. "I don't know how you can ask that after the stunts you've pulled this summer."

"I wouldn't have done any of that if you wouldn't treat me like a prisoner."

"That's a little melodramatic, don't you think?"

"I don't care." She got abruptly to her feet. The glow from the lamp out in the foyer touched her, highlighting the curls she flipped over her shoulder with such practiced ease. "I can't promise you there'll be no more stunts, Dad."

The defiance in her voice clubbed at him. "What do you mean?"

"You heard me."

Somehow, he had to make her understand. He fell back on the same old arguments. "Sammi, you're too young for Kirk Williams. You could end up involved in something that's way over your head."

"I wish you'd worry about your own sex life for a while."

He was used to her saucy talk, but that stunned him. "What?"

"Just what I said," she retorted. "Instead of spending all your time worrying about what I'm *not* doing, why don't you *do* something? Jeez, Dad, sometimes I think you're going to wind up with Sue Ann from the supermarket."

"You shouldn't be worrying about that."

"Sue Ann's just an example to show you could do a lot worse than Caroline."

Reid shook his head. "Go back to bed, Sammi."

Snorting in disgust, she started out of the room, but wheeled to face him once again in the doorway. "I just don't want you to be alone, Dad. You don't deserve to be alone."

But he was. And there were times, like now, when he felt as if he had always been on his own. All the most important people in his life always left him to carry on by himself. Even his daughter was slipping away. He wanted to hold on, to slow the march of time, but he knew he couldn't. He watched her leave the room, with her curls and her temper and her defiance, and felt he was losing her, losing a grip.

But she was right. He didn't want to be alone. He admitted that grudgingly, the same way he admitted one thing more.

He wished he hadn't sent Caroline away.

With all her baggage from the past. Even with the dragon she battled. He wished she was here.

That wish ate at him for days. Until he couldn't ignore it.

Caroline had her princess trapped in the harem of a brutal warlord in a land made of ice. Her knight had joined forces with the warlord, a ruse to help set her free. Her brother, the prince, who needed her strength, was fighting a losing battle at home. Time was running out. The ice and the snow of a strange world were sapping the princess's sanity, freezing her gift of foresight.

And Caroline was pleased by the torture she was inflicting on all her characters. She especially liked the ice. Princess Mai's prison had begun as a desert, but somehow, with the heat wave that was beating down on the Applewood Valley, ice had become much more appealing.

Caroline had been on a creative binge ever since leaving Reid's house several nights earlier. She needed to lose herself in the words, always her best refuge. She had to do something other than think about Reid and how foolish he had made her feel.

The only alternative to writing or thinking of the man who didn't want her was a pursuit of the dragon. But her elusive memories held no fascination for her these days.

After a month at home, she had done very few of the things she had planned to help the memories return. She couldn't make herself spend any significant time at the big house, where the memories were surely waiting. She hadn't gone into town to pick up a copy of the police report on her mother's car accident. She was building a wall against remembering as surely as her princess was holding her captor at bay. For the past few days, she had succeeded.

She just hoped the dragon couldn't climb the wall.

Sitting at her computer, with only a meager fan to combat the heat of a summer night, she wondered why she was still here in this steamy Tennessee valley when she could be home. In her pink house in Carmel, an ocean breeze would be blowing. The nights would be cool, with the heavy scent of gardenias wafting from the garden out back.

She sighed as she thought of that garden. She had bought the house right after her divorce. It was small and a little shabby, but she had fallen in love with the overgrown lot. Her ex-husband had laughed at her, told her she was still a farm girl at heart. And perhaps he was right, because she had taken such pleasure in digging in the dirt and coaxing things to grow.

But she had abandoned her flowers to come here. The beds were probably dying, untended and unloved by the lawn service she had found. She should go home and rescue them.

Home. Which way was home for her? She had known the first day she came back that this land, this valley, was the home of her heart. Here, she could feel the tug of her roots. But California was the place where she had run to when those roots proved too brittle to anchor her world. Would those roots hold this time? Could she know peace here? Or should she run again?

"Stop it," told herself out loud. She didn't want to think about it now. She wanted to write, to escape.

But her concentration was gone. The sentences wouldn't blend one into the other the way she needed them to. So she sat back in her straight-backed wooden chair and gave in to her most troubling thoughts.

She had made a idiot of herself with Reid. She should have known she couldn't go in pursuit of him that way. Pursuing wasn't her style. And he was a man who did things in his own time, his own way. Their one night of passion had been just what he said—an impulse, an aberration in his otherwise carefully constructed world. He had his rules, and he lived by them.

And she was Caroline Parrish, once forbidden to his brother, and now to him.

He was the last person she expected on her doorstep.

Yet when a sound on her porch made her turn from the computer, she found Reid standing on the other side of the screen door. She hadn't heard a car, wouldn't have thought of him if she had. But there was no mistaking his broad-shouldered figure silhouetted by the porch light.

Pleasure sent her to her feet. Caution made her hesitate halfway across the room.

"I wouldn't blame you if you locked me out," he said.

"Maybe I should."

Not waiting for an invitation, he pulled open the door and stepped inside. He held up a foil-wrapped plate. "I could put these brownies from Sammi out on the porch, but she'd be awful mad if a squirrel stole them."

The rumble of Caroline stomach reminded her that she hadn't eaten since sometime in the early afternoon when Lainey had forced some lunch on her. "Brownies?"

He held out the plate. "Sammi's best dish. A peace offering."

"I didn't know we were at war."

"She feels pretty bad about that scene the other night." He shuffled his feet, looking distinctly uncomfortable. "I do, too."

Dragging perspiration-dampened hair back from her forehead, Caroline regarded him with suspicion. "I didn't expect to see you."

"I didn't expect to be here."

"Why are you?"

"Because I couldn't stay away."

The words were rough-edged, as if they were torn from him without his consent, but they made hope bloom in Caroline's chest. He looked at her in a way that made her wish she had combed her hair in the past few hours. Or that she had put on some makeup. Or something a little more flattering than baggy denim shorts and a loose red tank top. He looked at her in a way that reminded her of the passion she had felt in his arms.

Nerves thrumming, she stepped forward and took the plate out of his hands. She kept her tone as light as possible. "I guess it would be a shame to turn you away when you've come bearing chocolate."

"Sammi said that'd do the trick."

They smiled at one another. A shy smile. Like two strangers on a blind date instead of strangers who had already skimmed into the depths of intimacy together.

"You want milk or coffee with these?" Caroline asked, turning toward the kitchen.

He caught her arm, drew her back. "I want this," he murmured, dipping his head to touch his lips to hers. The kiss grew and deepened, as was the norm with them, and the brownies were nearly lost to the floor.

Rescuing them, Reid said, "Make mine coffee."

Caroline's head was spinning so that it took a moment to know what he was talking about. But she recovered.

In the kitchen she brewed coffee and told herself to exercise some restraint, to keep in mind what had happened the other night at his house. Reid had treated her like a child, sending her away. Lying to her. Telling her that what had passed between them was just a mistake. But now here he was, offering kisses and words of apology. If he thought she would forget what had happened, that they would just crawl back into bed together, he was very mistaken.

Or was he?

With that question beating a rhythm in her head, she came back to the front room with the coffee and found Reid standing in front of her computer.

"You're working," he said, taking a steaming mug from her. "I don't want to interrupt."

"It's okay." She tapped a few commands into the keyboard to save her most recent work. "I was stuck, anyway."

"Isn't it going well?"

She was surprised because he sounded as if he really cared about the answer.

He lifted an eyebrow at her look. "What is it?"

"You haven't seemed very interested in what I do."

"I came to the library, didn't I?"

"Yes, but I thought that was just because Sammi wanted you to come."

He shrugged. "I was curious about your work. Sammi's been reading your stories for a couple of years now. I never dreamed those books she wouldn't put down were written by you."

"Maybe someday we'll be reading books by her."

Making no reply, he strolled to the sofa.

"I guess you wouldn't want Sammi to be a writer," Caroline said, following him.

"I want her to be secure and happy."

"That means writing fiction is out." Sitting down, she set her mug of coffee aside and took the foil off the plate of brownies he had placed on the coffee table trunk. "I don't know many writers who feel secure or happy for very much of the time."

Reid let that pass and sat back, studying her. "Lainey's worried about you."

"Lainey?" Caroline repeated, a brownie halfway to her mouth. "When did you talk to her?"

"She was grooming one of her horses up at the barn when I drove by. I stopped to talk, and left my truck up there."

"What did she say about me?"

"That you're working all the time. Not eating." He drained his coffee quickly, studying her over the rim of the mug. "She said she'd make me pay if I was the reason you looked like a ghost."

"Do I look that way?"

He leaned forward, capturing her chin with his fingertips. "Worn out, but not ready for a shroud just yet."

She pulled away, wishing once more for her makeup kit. "Gee, but your flattery is overwhelming."

"I've never been good with words."

"That's not true."

He held up a broad-palmed hand. A farmer's hand. Strong. Scarred. Blunt-fingered. Hardly elegant. "This is the only thing I've ever had to rely on. Maybe that's why I didn't understand Kev..." He paused, swallowed his brother's name, his hand closing into a fist and falling back to his side. "Maybe that's why I don't understand Sammi. She doesn't think like me."

Caroline downed the rest of the brownie and then cocked her head to the side, looking him over. "I've seen some similarities between the two of you. Like being headstrong and stubborn."

"She got all my worst faults."

"But taken in another context, those faults translate into qualities like determination and perseverance. You also have those in spades."

His eyes narrowed. "I guess I've had to be determined."

She knew that. He had assumed so many burdens at a young age. "You've had a lot of trouble, Reid."

"Life's full of trouble for everyone. I'm not special."

Shaking her head, Caroline dusted the brownie crumbs from her fingers. "Aunt Loretta was fond of telling Lainey and I that the Lord only gives you the amount of trouble he thinks you can bear."

Reid managed a grin and put his coffee cup on the trunk. "You and me, I guess we're a couple of the chosen ones."

She closed her eyes, shivering unexpectedly. "I think maybe I'm an exception. Because I've never felt especially strong."

Forgetting her resolution about holding back, she allowed Reid to slip his arm around her shoulders and pull her back against the soft, giving cushions of the sofa. It felt so good to lean on his strength. Until this moment she hadn't realized how desperately she had wanted to be in his arms these past few days. After a lifetime of running from a man's embrace, how quickly she had come to need it. It was all so fast. Too fast. That was part of the problem.

He whispered her name against her hair. "What am I doing here?" he asked.

She twisted to look at him. "You tell me."

"I should be home, with my daughter, making sure she doesn't do something foolish with that boy she can't stop seeing. I shouldn't have sent her over to her friend's so that I could come here. I shouldn't be here with you. I shouldn't want to spend the night with you in my arms."

That made Caroline pull away. "If you feel that way, maybe you should leave."

"I can't."

"Why?"

He got to his feet and walked away from her, then turned, his expression a study in torment. "I can't get you out of my head, Caroline. I can't stop wanting you."

Those words sent a surge of triumph through her, but she didn't move, tried not to betray how she felt. She wanted to hear all he had to say and felt.

Shoving an impatient hand through his hair, he scowled at her, hardly loverlike. "You want to know what's terrible? Sammi keeps defying me in order to be with this boy I know isn't good for her. She's going to keep defying me. She as much as told me so. But I know how she feels. Because I'm defying myself. To be with you."

Caroline pushed herself to the edge of the sofa. "And I'm not good for you?"

His laughter was short. "You're hell. Hell to resist."

"And you're used to resisting, aren't you?"

He let out a breath. "Yeah, I am used to resisting. All my life I've known how to walk away from what I knew was wrong. Oh, I made mistakes..." He held up his hand to cut off the protest he must have sensed from her. "I've made plenty of mistakes. Big ones. But I always knew in the end how to get through them, how to keep going, how to deal with the disappointment or the pain or the guilt ... or the temptation."

"You don't know how to deal with me?"

Once more a smile touched his stern mouth. "Oh, I know, all right. I know I should walk out that door. I've known I should walk away from you from the start. But I don't want to."

"What do you want?"

Heat simmered in his gaze. Pure sexual fire. He didn't need to say anything. Caroline knew what he wanted. And because she wanted the same, she crossed the room and went into his arms.

He had come to her, she thought, glorying in the knowledge. This stubborn, rigid man had come to her. In his own time. In his own way. He was here, and she was safe in his arms.

Caroline felt as if a window had been thrown open between them and she had peeked in at the workings of his mind. She had always known that he was a man who took life and his responsibilities seriously. She had thought him narrow in his view and controlling of others. And perhaps, in many respects he was all of those things. But she hadn't realized until these past few days just how firm a grip he kept on himself, as well. However strict a taskmaster he had been with others in his life, he was more so with himself. He walked a straight line.

She knew about narrow paths. She had lived most of her life in a tightly constrained world of her own making. To step outside the boundaries was too big a risk. It was only after her divorce, when she had sat in a garden that bloomed with life, that she had realized how empty her world really was—without passion, without love, without children or a man with whom to share her life and her home. It was only then that she had decided to venture outside the gate of her self-made prison.

Because she had faced fear of the unknown for so long, she knew just how much courage it had taken for

Reid to come to her tonight. He was going against his instincts. He was walking outside the boundaries.

She welcomed him in that first step. She pulled him forward with fervor. With kisses and sighs and touches that worked like a drug.

In return, he was her shield. Holding back the doubts. Sealing off the fears. Reid's touch was the best weapon she had ever found against the pain in her heart. More powerful than even the fantasies she wove in her mind and set down on paper, his touch filled her, soothed her.

They made love where they were, on the rag rug, with the door still open to the night. Without bothering to shed more than the most necessary of clothes. Without much more preamble than a kiss. Fast and hard and urgently, they soared and shattered together.

There would be time, Reid told her. Time for long hours of bliss. They took just such an hour in her bed. Then they slept. Sated. Naked. Tangled together on top of the sheets.

What cruel irony that the nightmares Caroline had been holding at bay picked that moment to return.

The dragon was back. With her mother in his jaws.

Chapter Eight

Caroline's scream tore through Reid's slumber like a knife, a deep, jagged cut that brought him instantly awake. Beside him, she was twisting and thrashing, fighting some unseen villain. The name she called was her grandfather's. She was screaming for him to stop.

Reid pulled her hard against his chest, rocked her, called to her, until she stopped fighting and her screams died in her throat. But she didn't stay in his arms. Dragging herself free with a muffled cry, she got out of bed and ran for the bathroom, where he heard her being violently, frighteningly ill.

Stopping at the half-closed door, he called her name.

Over the sound of running water, her reply was weak. "I'm all right. Just go back to bed."

Feeling helpless but unsure of what he should do, Reid snapped on the bedside lamp and pulled on his jeans. Going back to sleep wasn't an option, not with her bloodcurdling scream still echoing in his head. God in Heaven, what had her grandfather done to her? The most likely possibility Reid could think of made him sick.

The bathroom door squeaked behind him and he turned as Caroline stepped out. While fiddling with the tie of her robe, she tried to smile. "I guess rich chocolate and coffee on an empty stomach wasn't such a good idea."

"Come here." He took her hand and guided her to the bed. She sat on the edge. He knelt on one knee in front of her and searched her pale, strained features. "It wasn't chocolate that made you scream like that."

"Did I scream?"

He folded his hand over the fingers she had clenched in her lap. "You know you did."

"It was just a nightmare."

"About your grandfather."

She looked at him in surprise. "How did you know?"

"You called his name, asked him to stop."

Shuddering, she closed her eyes.

Gently he took her chin in his hand and forced her to look at him. "What was he doing?"

She wouldn't—or couldn't—tell him.

Dropping her hands, Reid got slowly to his feet. He didn't know how to phrase what he was about to ask. He sure didn't know if this was the right time or place to ask. But he had to do it. So he sucked in his breath and plunged in. "Did your grandfather molest you, Caroline?"

Her head jerked up. Her denial was an emphatic "No!"

"But from what I've read, seen on television and what you've told me, and now with this nightmare, I thought maybe he could have—"

"He didn't," Caroline told him, getting to her feet.

"Are you sure?"

"Yes," she restated, but then she wavered, chewing on her bottom lip. "At least, I think I'm sure."

"It's not something I bring up lightly, Caroline."

"I know that. And you're not the first person to suggest it. Over the years, several experts have been certain that abuse was at the root of all my problems. The panic attacks. The fears. The nightmares." Briefly she closed her eyes. "Even the aversion I had to my husband's touch."

The last was news to Reid. She had welcomed his touch, gloried in it. And yet there was an innocence to her response, an attitude of discovery that had accompanied each sensual peak they had scaled.

She wasn't pausing to explain any of that. "I never felt that Grandfather did anything to me," she reaffirmed, shaking her head. "I'm just sure that's something I would know. Down deep. Down here." She put a hand to her stomach.

"But you've blocked out the night your mother died. Why not that, too?"

She started to protest again, but then stopped, dropping back to the bed with a weary sigh. "Oh, hell, Reid, maybe that is what happened. God knows,

Grandfather was cruel and bitter. Maybe he was depraved, as well.'' The last words caught on a sob. But she pressed a fist to her mouth, took a deep breath and brought herself under control.

Reid felt as if his heart was twisting inside out as he watched her obvious pain. But he thought she should talk about this, try to remember. No matter how painful the truth might be, surely it was better than a mystery that ate at her soul.

''It could be true,'' he said gently. ''You were afraid of your grandfather.''

''That's what doesn't fit, Reid. I wasn't afraid.''

He stared at her, confused. ''Wait a minute. The night you and Kevin came to me, when I took you home to your grandfather, you were scared to death.''

''But I didn't know what I was frightened of. Remember?''

She was right. One of the most frustrating aspects of that night had been that she couldn't put a name or a face or a description to what she had feared. It was only this summer, when they had been arguing about that night, that she said she realized her grandfather was at the root of her fears. She had realized only days ago that Robert Parrish was the dragon in her dreams.

''I hated Grandfather,'' she whispered now. ''But I didn't fear him.''

''Why did you hate him?''

''Because he hated me.''

''Surely—''

''Oh, but he did,'' she insisted. ''I was this half Native American creature my mother had brought into his home and his precious family. He despised me, despised her for having me."

Reid had always known that Robert Parrish hadn't approved of his daughter's marriage. It had been common knowledge here in the valley, and judging from the gossip he had heard from Sue Ann and Marge at the supermarket earlier this summer, most of the county knew the details of Linda Parrish's brief foray into matrimony. But to say Robert had despised her for it or hated Caroline because of her parentage, was quite a stretch from disapproval.

"He didn't seem to hate you," Reid pointed out. "That last summer when you and Kevin kept defying us both and seeing each other, he came over and told me to keep my brother away from you. He said you were a Parrish, too good for the likes of us McClures."

She gave an indelicate snort. "Oh, he wanted a little Parrish to show the world. He tried to make believe I was what he wanted. He tried to make sure I behaved the way he thought a Parrish should. But mostly, he just loathed me. That's why I didn't fear him. I loathed him back."

"It sounds..." Reid wasn't sure he could put a word to the cold picture of family life her words painted. The image he had always carried of her as a pampered, rich little girl was rapidly evaporating.

"If it weren't for Uncle Coy and Aunt Loretta, I'm sure I would have been even more screwed up than I was."

"I always thought they were good people," Reid murmured. "But although they were neighbors, I can't say I knew them too well. They kept to themselves."

"Because Grandfather told them to, and he controlled us all."

"Coy could have taken his family and left."

"Left this valley? It would have killed him." Her laugh was bitter. "But he should have. He shouldn't have taken what Grandfather dished out. Grandfather treated him like dirt. He always claimed Coy wasn't really his half brother."

Reid was amazed. "Anyone looking at them would know they had the same father."

"Grandfather was grown when his father remarried. When Coy was born, he knew he would have to share what was left of the family fortune with him. Grandfather did everything he could to freeze Coy out."

"That's why Coy lived down here instead of up at the big house," Reid murmured, suddenly understanding a living arrangement he had once chalked up to eccentricity.

"Grandfather treated him like a farmhand."

"But Coy took it."

"He loved working this land more than he hated his half brother, more than he cared about living up there or about money. This farm was Coy's life."

Sorting through the layers of family secrets and hatred was an overwhelming task for Reid, whose own family had been so simple by comparison. "What about your mother?" he asked after several moments of silence. "Why did she stay here with your grandfather if he hated you both? Why didn't she leave with your father?"

"I don't know. I never knew what happened between my parents except that I'm sure my grandfather engineered it. One morning my father and brother were here, the next they were gone."

"You remember them leaving? But you were only three or so."

She looked down at her hands. "Maybe it's more a dream than a memory, but I remember it being hot the day they left. Adam and I were playing outside. Our father came and got him, and they left in a truck. Dust blew up from under the wheels as they drove away. Adam waved to me from the back window."

"And you never saw him again," Reid completed softly.

There was a curiously emotionless quality to her voice as she continued. "Sometime later my mother told me they were dead. Nothing was ever right again."

"It seems like your mother could have just taken you and left. She was an educated person, wasn't she? Couldn't she have survived somewhere else, away from your grandfather?"

Caroline looked him straight in the eye. "You said it best years ago, Reid, when you accused me of being just like her. Mother was nuts."

He took a step forward, suddenly ashamed. "Caroline—"

"Don't apologize for the truth," she returned in a flat tone. "Mother was already lost in her own world before she discovered bourbon. Afterward, she was even worse."

"Your grandfather drove her to that?"

"The drinking started when he wanted her to get married again."

"Why?"

"He badgered her," Caroline said, her eyes narrowing. "He said she had to find a new husband, a suitable husband. Preferably a rich husband. By the time I was ten or so, the mill our family used to own was failing. I suppose Grandfather wanted cash to keep it going. A good marriage by mother might have helped."

Reid knew the textile mill, which still stood empty at the edge of town, had been the source of the Parrish family fortune. Though the Parrishes had settled here as farmers, an enterprising member had branched out into manufacturing. At one time they had owned half the businesses in town. But the family fortunes had dwindled to just the textile mill and Applewood Farm.

Some folks said Robert Parrish ran the mill into the ground with his high-handed ways. Whatever the case, its loss, coming on the heels of Linda's death and Caroline's running away, seemed to suck the life right out of him. When he died, the farm had been all that remained, and Reid knew that for years it had been a struggle for Coy Parrish to hold on to the land.

Caroline was staring off into the distance, her eyes wide with pain and memories. "Grandfather said he wanted her to remarry and have another child. A child by someone respectable, instead of a dirty Indian."

"You heard him say that?" Reid couldn't fathom such cruelty to a child. But evidently Robert Parrish was cut from a cloth far different from most decent people.

"I heard," Caroline whispered. "I knew how he felt."

She could remember crouching high up in the shadows of the staircase above the broad hall at the big house, listening to her grandfather plan for a grandchild he wouldn't be ashamed of, a grandchild without her father's black hair and Cherokee features. And she remembered how she had hated him for that, hated him for hating her.

Reid sat down on the bed and took her hand between both of his. "But your mother didn't get married."

"No, she got revenge." Words, half formed and elusive flitted through Caroline's head. She frowned, trying to recall them. When they came to her, she spoke them aloud without thinking. "Mother just got drunk and picked up men. Any old man would do. As long as he was exactly the opposite of what Grandfather wanted for her."

"What?" Reid said, eyes widening.

Caroline could feel the blood drain from her face as the meaning of the words sank in. "How do I know that?" she demanded of Reid. "How do I know that's what Mother did?"

"Did your grandfather tell you that?"

"I don't know. I don't think ..." She got to her feet and paced away, a fist of pain and denial forming in her chest. But she knew the truth. It was her mother who had told her about the men. Caroline could see her mother's face, hear her voice. But when? When would she have said such a thing to her? It had to have been the night she died. But where? Why? Was that the reason they had been in the car together when Grandfather tried to stop them?

The memory was waiting for her. But the harder she tried to reach it, the further away it slipped.

But other memories crashed around her.

The rain was pounding the car. Thunder was booming. Lightning flashing. And her mother was screaming while her grandfather ran beside the car, reaching in, bellowing...

"Oh, God," Caroline whispered. "God, just stop." She had blocked these memories for days now. She was determined to block them now.

Reid came up behind her, settling gentle hands on her shoulders. She turned into his arms. "It's all so ugly, Reid. So awful. I don't want to know anything else. Whatever it is that I don't remember, I just don't want to know any longer."

"You told me that before. Down by the creek. You told me you were thinking about going home and forgetting about trying to remember what happened."

"And you said I'd regret leaving."

"I still believe that."

She pressed her face into his chest. "It hurts so damn much. I'm sick of hurting."

But Reid wouldn't let her off the hook so easily. He held her away from him, his dark eyes intent on hers. "Tell me what you dreamed tonight."

She resisted, looked away.

Somewhere in the darkest part of her mind, the dragon reared up with her mother in his grasp.

But she wouldn't think of that. She didn't want to know that.

Reid said, "Tell me about the dream. Maybe I can help you see something that will spark your memory."

"No."

"Caroline..."

She twisted out of his reach. "I said no. I don't want to talk about it. I don't want to think about it."

"But that's the only way you'll remember."

"Didn't you hear me just a minute ago? I don't want to remember."

"Then you'll never be free."

Caroline turned away from him, as if that would negate the truth in his quiet words. But in the warped and spotty old mirror that hung above a scarred dresser, she could see their reflections. There she was, her eyes full of fright, with Reid behind her, broad-shouldered and strong, ready to slay dragons. Only this wasn't really his fight. It was hers. And she didn't want to pursue monsters. Not tonight. Maybe not ever. She wasn't strong enough to do battle any longer.

Conceding a final defeat wasn't easy for Caroline. She had begun this summer with such hope. But it had only carried her so far. She had won some victories. *Reid* was a victory. She had triumphed in his arms. And tonight, he had come to her. That joy was more important than the sharp edges of her memories.

She turned to him again. "I am free," she said with quiet insistence. "Every time you touch me, I'm set free."

"That's not enough."

"Shouldn't I be the judge of that?"

"You need to remember."

She closed her eyes and shut out the voice inside that told her he was right. She shut out everything but the certainty that what she needed most was the sweet oblivion he could offer with his touch. She wanted him so much. She had to show him how much.

Feeling audacious, she unknotted the tie of her robe, then dropped the garment to the floor.

She saw Reid's reaction. Desire darkened his eyes, made his powerful chest expand and contract with his quickened breathing. His gaze slipped over her, lingering, filling with hunger. Her nipples hardened under that gaze. Her pulse raced. Her own desire unfurled with liquid heat in her belly.

But even as a rosy flush spread over her body, she kept her head high, her eyes on him. "I couldn't do this before," she murmured. "Before you, I could never have stood here like this."

Reid didn't want to be glad. He wasn't quite the Neanderthal his daughter claimed he was. He had never gotten off on thoughts of being the first or the only with any woman. Yet he had to admit there was something damned erotic about knowing Caroline had never been able to show her passion to any other man. He was glad no one else had seen her this way, proudly naked, offering herself so sweetly.

"No one," she repeated, stepping toward him. Her hands went to the zipper of his jeans. Slowly she drew it down, reached inside. "No one else ever made me this bold, Reid. Not anyone but you."

Not her husband. Not Kevin. Reid believed that. He wanted to believe everything she said. And he wanted to accept that his touch might really be enough to heal the raw wounds inside her. He knew he was a strong man. A good man. But he didn't know if being strong and good was enough to help Caroline defeat her dragon.

And yet how could he force her to confront something so horrible? Her mind had sealed this knowledge from her. Maybe he didn't have any right to push her to move past that seal. His only rights were the ones she granted him now. All he could do tonight was give her what she said she needed. He could take what she offered in return. For tonight, it was enough.

Reid wasn't fool enough to believe that it would last.

The summer, so damp through the middle of July, turned hot and dry as the calendar slipped into August. Grass crackled underfoot. Flies swarmed on cattle. Air conditioners sputtered and failed. Perspiration glistened on faces that turned heavenward in search of a rain cloud.

Reid knew he should have been worried about the effect of the heat on milk production. He should have concerned himself with figuring out a way to replace the tractor that wouldn't stay repaired. He should have been suspicious of Sammi, who was low-key and agreeable these days. But he was none of those things. In the midst of a drought, he was a drowning man. Drowning in Caroline.

Passion ruled his life. He was old enough to know passion could cloud a man's mind. But he didn't care. He wanted to be with Caroline. In bed. Out of it. He had spent all his forty-five years being sensible and prudent. He was claiming this last month of this summer as his own personal insanity.

It wasn't just the sex, although that was spectacular. His happiness came from knowing there was someone waiting to be with him at the end of a long day. To ask him what had happened. To commiserate over the heat. To rub the ache in his lower back. It was the ordinary moments with Caroline that he cherished most. He liked it that most nights Caroline was at his house, making dinner with him and Sammi. Other nights, he joined her for a sandwich at her place. Or they went into town for supper and a movie. Or they just sat on the porch and stared at the moon.

There were out-of-the-ordinary times, as well. One early August night they spent in the barn with Lainey, with a collie who was struggling to deliver her pups. One Saturday they braved several hours in a car full of teenagers, to take Sammi and her friends on a shopping trip to Chattanooga for back-to-school clothes. And on one memorable Sunday, they rode Lainey's two best horses up the old logging road and over the ridge to the next valley. The ride was beautiful, but the memorable part came from their stiff legs and saddle sores.

But even that didn't keep them from making love. They indulged whenever or wherever they could snatch a moment of privacy. In the apple orchard on a lazy Saturday evening. Down by the creek at midday. For one long, special and private evening at his house.

Reid learned a lot of little things about Caroline during these weeks. She cried at sappy commercials. She hated to cook. She sprinkled Parmesan cheese on her popcorn. And a kiss on the inner part of her thigh was as effective as fifteen minutes of any other fore-play.

But of the memories that were held prisoner deep in her mind, he learned nothing new.

She still had nightmares she wouldn't share with him. She had quiet times, moments when he knew she was puzzling through the bits and pieces that had come back to her about the night her mother died.

Though she was resisting, Reid knew she had to re-member. She would never know peace until she re-membered. He had to help, even though doing so risked the harmony they were enjoying.

He had tried to view this time they had together as simply a page separated from the book of the rest of their lives. But he was smart enough to know that one page had very little meaning when taken out of con-text. There were chapters that had come before now. And the ending had yet to be written. Sooner or later Reid knew Caroline's story had to be ended.

He was thinking of stories, the ones Caroline had told him about her family, when he drove up to the big house at Applewood on a Friday late in August. Drawing to stop in the back driveway, he stared up at the big red brick structure. The eaves and shutters were painted a clean, crisp white. Neatly trimmed shrubs and bright flowers ran along the sides. Lainey kept the place looking tidy and inviting.

But Reid had to wonder what Caroline saw when she looked at these windows and these walls.

A dragon's lair?

The description drew a brief smile. He had dragons on the mind since Caroline had convinced him to read the manuscript she had completed last weekend. He hadn't wanted to read it, fearing he would hate it and would feel compelled to lie, something he didn't do very well. But the story had captured his interest from the first page. The characters were likable and believable, the action intense. And in the end, without help from a prince or a knight, Caroline's fictional princess had defeated her dragon.

But Caroline still needed help with her own nemesis. In the papers Reid now held in his hand, he hoped to have found a way to assist her. Tucking the plain manila envelope under his arm, he went into the kitchen where Lainey, Caroline and Sammi were canning the last tomatoes of the season.

He wasn't surprised to see that Lainey had managed to supervise the whole process without destroying her immaculate kitchen. Sammi was at the stove, watching the gauge on a big pressure cooker. Caroline was washing some pots at the sink. In the center of the room, with a satisfied gleam in her eyes, Lainey was inspecting a tableful of canned tomatoes.

"Would you look at this?" the redhead said, holding one of the glass jars toward Reid. "Even without much rain, these are some of the prettiest tomatoes I ever grew."

Sammi rolled her eyes. "I think the prettiest tomatoes are the ones you buy in cans at the store. With those, you don't have to think about how much trouble went into them."

"I guess you're not destined to be a farm wife." Teasingly, Reid tugged at one of the curls straggling from a lopsided topknot and down his daughter's back. Then he went over to Caroline to claim a kiss.

"Isn't it a little warm in here for that stuff?" Sammi's delighted grin belied the tartness of her tone. She made no secret of her pleasure over Reid's involvement with Caroline.

Laughing, Lainey pretended to fan herself. "If you ask me, these two are used to heat."

While Reid leaned on the counter next to her, Caroline tsk-tsked in her cousin's direction. "That's a fine way to talk in front of an impressionable teenager. We'll just see if I come up here to help you can green beans and tomatoes or make blackberry jelly again."

Lainey, who continued to check the seals on the jars of tomatoes, looked unconcerned. "You'll have forgotten that vow by the time the garden comes in next spring."

Quite innocently, Sammi asked, "Do you think you'll be here next spring, Caroline?"

In the silence that followed, the pressure valve on the slow cooker began to whistle, saving Caroline from a reply. Lainey and Sammi dealt with the last batch of tomatoes while she scrubbed a pot in the sink and studiously avoided looking at Reid. Why, she couldn't say. The issue of her staying or not hadn't come up.

It wasn't fair of her to be piqued because he hadn't come out and asked about her plans. More than him, she had been playing a game of take-it-one-day-at-a-time. Since she had decided to stop trying to retrieve her elusive and troubling memories, she had been living for the moment.

Not that the memories had left her alone. Quite the contrary. They plagued her dreams and edged in at other moments, as well, especially on her infrequent trips up here to the big house. She hadn't been in the house more than three or four times recently, and hadn't gone past the kitchen at all. She was afraid, so terribly afraid of walking around a corner and running right into a past she no longer cared to recall.

Reid thought she should be trying to remember. He was such a straightforward person. If he had a problem, he formulated a plan and worked toward a solution. But he just didn't understand how painfully impossible this had become for her. The horrible truths she already knew about her family were enough. She had reached her limit on acceptance. She preferred living with the mystery. She had done it long enough to cope.

And besides, the past month had brought her so much to be happy about. Why spoil it?

Chancing a look at Reid, she saw that he was smiling as he listened to the extensive sixteenth birthday wish list Sammi was relating to Lainey. He looked good, she thought. Younger, more rested, happier than he had seemed at the beginning of the summer. Their relationship had been good for him. Good for all of them, she thought, glancing at the pretty teenager across the kitchen.

She and Sammi had become the best of friends. In recent weeks, they had moved from superficial topics to some deeper discussions. About a boy named Kirk, for the most part.

Though Caroline certainly didn't encourage Sammi concerning Kirk, she did listen. Sammi claimed he was nothing like his reputation. He was cocky, yes. But sensitive, too. And reading between the lines of what the girl said, Caroline thought half of Kirk's past troubles were because he was a weapon in a continuing battle between his divorced parents. Whatever the case, Kirk was needy and forbidden, an irresistible combination for a girl like Sammi, who reached out to others with such an open heart. In that respect more than any other, she reminded Caroline of her Uncle Kevin. And maybe Kirk was a little like Caroline had been at that age.

Caroline frowned at the comparison as she reached for another pot to wash. She wouldn't wish history to repeat itself. She wished Reid would sit down and talk to Sammi about her feelings for Kirk. The girl needed someone to listen to her. She needed her father to set aside his preconceived notions and be objective.

But objectivity wasn't one of Reid's best qualities. And Caroline recognized his limitations, no matter how much she loved him.

And she did love him. That certainty had been growing inside of her for weeks. She loved Reid McClure. Because he was strong and brave, unflinching in his loyalties, direct in his approach to life. She smiled, glancing sideways at him again. The qualities that made her love him were also the ones that infuriated her at times.

He turned, caught her looking at him and laughed. "What's the matter? Have the fumes off these tomatoes gotten to you?"

She forced a laugh around the emotion that tightened her throat. She wondered that he could look at her and not see the love in her eyes. "It's not the tomatoes," she told him. "It's you." Disregarding her wet hands, or their audience, she kissed him.

"They're at it again," Sammi said with typical disdain. "Like rabbits, or something."

Reid sent her a mock-serious glower. "You'd better watch that smart mouth, Cookie. There's still time to cancel your birthday party."

His mention of the party drew Caroline a meaningful look from Sammi. Groaning inwardly, Caroline turned back to the sink. Today Sammi had asked Caroline to test the waters with Reid about Kirk coming to her party. Though at first Caroline had advised the girl to forget it, Sammi had eventually worn her down.

There were an infinite number of other subjects she'd rather discuss with Reid. Starting with the fact that she was hopelessly, completely in love with him. She wondered exactly what he and everyone else in the room would say if she just announced her feelings. Smothering that crazy impulse, she grinned down at the dishwater.

"You look like someone with a secret," Reid told her.

She moved slightly, bumping her hip against his, smiling flirtatiously, but before she could say anything, Lainey's voice made her glance over her shoulder.

"Sammi," the redhead said, "there's an old wicker table upstairs that I'd like you to have for your birthday if you want it. It needs some paint, but since you've redone some other wicker pieces for your bedroom, I thought you might be able to work with this one, too."

"That sounds great," Sammi replied eagerly. "Can we go look at it now?"

"Sure." Setting the last jar of tomatoes down, Lainey looked at Caroline. "Why don't you come up and look at it with us? There may be something up there that you want."

Go upstairs? The very thought sent chills down Caroline's spine and chased away the glow of love she had been feeling. She hadn't been upstairs since that first week she'd been back. And there wasn't anything here that she wanted. The box Lainey had found with the picture of Caroline and Adam with their parents was still sitting on the pine sideboard. She didn't want even that.

"I'll just finish up here," she said, quickly turning back to the sink.

"Suit yourself," Lainey said as she followed Sammi through the doorway to the back hall.

Frowning now, Caroline scrubbed out the last pot, rinsed and placed it in the drain tray. Then she looked up at Reid. He was watching her, his expression thoughtful.

"What do you think would happen if you went upstairs?" he asked quietly.

It was odd realizing how well he had read her. Instead of answering, she sent the water down the drain and reached for a sponge.

But Reid wouldn't let up that easily. "Somewhere down deep, I don't believe you like not being able to do a simple thing like go up to the second floor of this house."

"You don't understand."

"No, I don't." His angry tone made her look at him again. "I don't think of you as a coward."

"I'm not."

"But you continue to be controlled by this. Why would you want that?"

Unwilling to argue with him about it, Caroline put all her energy into scrubbing out the sink with the sponge. Reid stood silently by until she was finished and had dried her hands on a towel.

"I have something for you," he said, holding out a manila envelope. "Something you should read."

She regarded it with the same trepidation she might have viewed a snake. "What is it?"

"Just open it."

"Not until you tell me what it is," she retorted, rapidly growing more than irritated with him.

"All right," he muttered, looking disgusted. "I called a friend of mine at the sheriff's office last week. It took a little time, but they found the report Sheriff Leavitt wrote on the night your mother was killed. This is it."

Caroline stared at the envelope again, her heart beginning to pound.

"Your answers could be in here," Reid said.

"I don't care."

"Yes, you do."

That pushed her irritation into downright anger. "Don't tell me how I feel, Reid. You have no idea what it's like to feel the way I do."

"All right," he muttered, ripping open one end of the envelope. "If you won't take it, then I'll just read it for you."

She started for the door. "I'm not going to listen, so you might as well save your breath."

"You have to listen. If you don't, you won't know what to ask Sheriff Leavitt when he gets here."

That made her stop and turn around. "Sheriff Leavitt is coming here?"

"After I got the report, I called and told him that you needed to talk to him about it. He's coming out."

Anger scorched through her. Damn this stubborn, direct man who thought he knew what was right for everyone. "You had no right, Reid. No right to get this report or call Leavitt and ask him to come and see me. You can just call him up and tell him to stay home."

"That'll be hard."

"Why?"

"Because he's coming up the back stairs right now."

She turned on her heel just as Sheriff Leavitt knocked on the back porch's windowed door.

Chapter Nine

Pride kept Caroline from running away from Sheriff Leavitt. If she left, he would think she was as crazy as her mother had been. And while it shouldn't matter what a man she barely knew thought of her, she couldn't help herself. How ironic that all her grandfather's admonishments not to disgrace the family name were finally bearing fruit.

Lainey came downstairs right after Leavitt appeared. She took over in her usual warm, hospitable way, clearing the kitchen table of canned tomatoes, pouring ice tea and serving some of her homemade gingerbread. She even volunteered to take Sammi home with the wicker table from upstairs.

Caroline would have preferred that Reid be the one to go. She was furious with him. Hands clenched in her lap, she sat at the table while he and Leavitt rambled on about the weather and other assorted inanities. The four-page report Reid had brought from the sheriff's office lay in the middle of the table, untouched, while the tension inside Caroline soared.

Finally she could stand it no more. She tapped the report and with ill-concealed impatience demanded, "Can we please get to this?"

Leavitt cocked one of his bristling gray eyebrows at her, then looked at Reid. "She went out to California and picked up some big city ways, didn't she?"

Caroline forced herself to sit back in her chair. "I'm sorry. I'm not trying to be rude."

"That's okay," the older man said, patting her hand. "I guess you've just forgotten that folks around here like to back into things, easy like."

"Yes, I know, but—"

"But she really wants to hear everything that happened the night her mother died," Reid cut in. His expression challenging her to deny that. "It's important to her."

The former sheriff was suddenly all business. He straightened his shoulders, put on his glasses and picked up the report. "I don't know what I can tell you that's not in here. Like I said at your library talk, Caroline, I came along right after the accident happened."

He went on to outline facts Caroline had always known. Her mother's car had careened off the driveway and hit the stone wall and the oak tree. Caroline had been thrown free of the car and had been unconscious when Leavitt arrived. Her mother, who had also been thrown out of the car, was dead, apparently of severe head trauma. The coroner's report had confirmed that later.

"So she hit the windshield first, then was thrown free?" Reid asked.

Leavitt consulted the report again. "It was hard to tell just what had happened at first. It was storming to beat the band. Rain like you wouldn't believe. And I was mainly concerned with Caroline, because she was still alive, and I needed to get someone out here to help her."

She could see his face looming over her, feel the rain and thunder.

Despite that sudden rush of memory, Caroline struggled to be as calm as the sheriff. "I do remember regaining consciousness," she said. "I remember you."

He shrugged. "If you say you did, Caroline, then I guess you did. But I don't remember you coming to, and from what I've written here, I certainly didn't think you had."

"What about Caroline's mother?" Reid interrupted. "She hit the windshield and then what?"

"The windshield was cracked but not broken. Then she apparently bounced out of the car, just as Caroline did. When the front end hit the rock wall, Caroline's door must have sprung open. Either that, or she tried to get out of the car before it hit the rocks."

"And her mother?"

"Same thing. As she was thrown free, Linda struck her head on a rock."

The words were straightforward, not descriptive or gory. Yet they piled up on Caroline, as wet and cold as the stone wall must have been the night her mother died.

Reid took the report and flipped through the pages, reading silently. "It says here that Robert Parrish admitted he had run down the driveway and tried to stop the car."

Running, reaching, bellowing in the rain . . .

Hands fisting on the table in front of her, Caroline held the memory at bay.

Leavitt cleared his throat and looked at Caroline apologetically. "I don't know if you know this, but we had picked your mother up for drunk driving on several occasions prior to that night."

"But what about this night?" Reid pressed.

"Robert Parrish said she was drunk, and blood alcohol tests later confirmed it. He told me he and his daughter had been arguing, and he had run after the car, trying to get her to stop. He said he knew she was in no condition to be driving, especially in that storm."

"You stole my boy. You took my Adam."

Her mother's angry, terrified voice swelled in Caroline's head. But she swept it away as quickly as she brushed away the perspiration that had gathered on her upper lip. It was an effort to keep herself in the present, at the table with Reid and the sheriff. She was being pulled into the memories, the horrible memories. Pulled in the same way she had been pulled that other night here in this kitchen when Reid had come to the door and startled her.

Why was Reid doing this? Couldn't he see she couldn't stand it?

But Reid didn't seem to notice. "Why was Caroline in the car?" he asked the sheriff as he turned over the last page of report.

"Doesn't it say why?"

"I don't see it."

Frowning, Leavitt took the report and leafed through it again. "Maybe I didn't ask why. There had been a family argument. I suppose I just assumed that Caroline got in the car with her mother. Don't you remember why?" he asked, turning to Caroline.

Reid answered for her. "As I told you, Caroline doesn't remember much about that night."

"I can't say that I'd want to remember it," Leavitt said, again shaking his head.

Caroline opened her mouth to tell him that she really didn't, but Reid cut her off. "Sheriff Leavitt, was there anything suspicious about that night?"

"Suspicious?"

"Strange. Unusual."

Shifting in his chair, the older man smoothed a hand through his thick crown of white hair, his brow knitting. "It was a horror. That's all I can say about it."

"A horror?" Reid repeated.

Leavitt gestured toward Caroline. "Here was this beautiful young girl, unconscious on the ground in that storm. And over there was her mother, dead, senselessly dead, in Robert Parrish's arms."

A picture clicked through Caroline's brain.

The dragon with her mother in his grasp.

She fought off a wave of nausea.

Reid said, "In his arms? I don't remember reading that in the report."

"I probably didn't put it that way," Leavitt retorted. "That's not how you would put it in a report." Seizing the papers again, he scanned them until he found what he was looking for. "It's right here. I said he was holding a woman, whom I was able to identify as his daughter. He told me she was dead. I confirmed that there was no pulse, then I went to see about Caroline."

The former sheriff laid the papers down again. He sat back in his chair, not quite as tall and straight as he had been only a moment before. Behind his glasses, his eyes were solemn, sad. He looked suddenly old. "I've never been able to forget that night. Especially the way Robert Parrish looked, sitting there in the rain on the ground, crying, rocking his daughter in his arms."

Caroline pushed away from the table and stood so abruptly that she overturned her chair and her glass of tea. Startled, Reid grabbed the glass, though not before the tea spread across the report. Caroline was pale, her features drawn.

"I have to go," she said, backing toward the door.

Sheriff Leavitt pulled off his glasses, looking confused.

Reid got to his feet. "Caroline—"

Still backing away, she stuttered, "Th-thank you for ... for coming, Sheriff." She backed right into the pine sideboard and sent a green box crashing to the floor, its contents spilling out. But she didn't pause to pick it up. She threw open the door and fled across the back porch without looking back.

Two long steps brought Reid to the doorway, where he was just in time to see Caroline sprint across the well-tended lawn toward the driveway and her little house down the hill. Sharp-edged guilt cut into him. He shouldn't have sprung this visit with Sheriff Leavitt on her without warning. He should have known it was impossible for her to have a calm discussion of the events of the night her mother died.

Hesitating, he glanced back at Leavitt, who murmured, "Too many years in California, I guess. Folks out there don't have any manners."

"I'd better go after her," Reid told him. The sheriff waved him off with the assurance that he would let himself out.

But as Reid started out the door, his boot hit the cardboard box Caroline had knocked off the sideboard. He knelt to pick it up, and a photograph caught his eye. A black-and-white shot of two happy people holding two plump, smiling babies.

Caroline's parents with her and her twin.

Staring down at that photograph, Reid knew a moment's unease, a funny prickle at the back of his neck. A sudden compulsion made him jerk around, but there was only Sheriff Leavitt in the kitchen, helping himself to another slice of Lainey's gingerbread.

But who else would he expect to see?

Silently cursing his foolishness, Reid shoved the photograph and everything else back in the box, then put it back on the sideboard on his way out the door. He had to get to Caroline to try to make amends.

Caroline was gasping for breath by the time she made it through the door of her house. She hadn't meant to run all the way home in the heat. But she had known she had to get out of that house, escape those memories.

Except that she hadn't escaped.

In the center of the room, she made a slow turn. She could feel the press of memories even here. They waited in the corners. They crouched behind closed doors. They tried to slide through the open screened windows. The horror of those memories was as thick as the hot, humid air.

She had to get away, run away from the pain.

There had been another hot day like this. Another day in August when she had known she couldn't live with the terror of living here at Applewood. That day she had run. Run as if the hounds of hell were at her feet.

Dear God, why had she ever come back?

Footsteps sounded on the porch, and Reid slammed through the screen door. Obviously winded, he braced his hands on his knees and bent forward from the waist before demanding, "Are you all right?"

Anger sent blood pounding to her pulse points. "As if you care."

"What does that mean?" Straightening, he caught her elbow.

She pulled back. "Don't play innocent with me. You had to have known I couldn't just sit there and listen to that man talk about Grandfather that way...about him holding Mother in his arms." She squeezed her eyes shut to blot out the picture the sheriff's words had conjured.

Reid said, "I thought—"

"Yes, *you* thought," she cut in. "You always think you know best, don't you?"

"I'm trying to help you."

"That's always your excuse, isn't it? You're always trying to do what you think is right for everyone. That's exactly what you did with—" Caroline bit her lip before the angry, accusatory words could slip out. Furious as she was, she had enough control not to drag Kevin into this. Regardless of how their relationship had deepened and changed, Reid's brother was still a subject they avoided at all cost.

"I'm sorry," Reid said quietly. "I wasn't thinking when I invited Sheriff Leavitt out here."

"Obviously not."

"But..." He hesitated, then plunged ahead. "But it did make you remember something, didn't it?"

"No."

Reid's gaze sharpened as he stepped closer and took her arm again. "Are you sure?"

"Damn you, Reid, I said no," Caroline retorted, pushing against his chest as she tried to get around him.

But he wouldn't let her. He held her steady, his gaze intent on her face. A face she tried to keep as blank as she could.

"You're lying," he muttered.

Now she jerked free. "And what if I am?"

"I don't care if you lie to me. But can you lie to yourself?"

His question made the room close around her. She was boxed in, and the walls were buckling, cracking beneath the force of what he wanted her to confront, what she could see in her mind's eye. . . .

The dragon with her mother in his arms, but looking at Caroline, seeing that she wasn't dead.

Caroline broke free of the image by sheer force of will, a will that was growing ragged and thin. The dragon's breath was blowing through cracks in her walls.

Her breath hitched in her throat, and Reid was instantly beside her, his eyes concerned, his touch gentle. But that wasn't enough. He could no longer help her forget.

"I have to get out of here," Caroline whispered.

He took hold of her hand.

"I have to leave."

"Then let's go."

She looked up at him. Into the eyes of the man she loved. His strong, even features made her falter, but couldn't break her resolve. "I don't mean leave this room. I mean the farm, this valley."

Reid might have chalked those words up to panic. But Caroline seemed suddenly dead calm. The composed look in her eyes rocked him back on his feet.

"I don't think I can stay here any longer," she continued. "If I stay, I'll remember—"

"But that's good."

"How do you know that?" she challenged.

"Because knowing what happened is the key to the rest of your life."

She paused for just half a beat. "Or to insanity."

"Caroline," he chided. "You know you don't believe that."

Sizzling with anger, her gaze locked onto his. "There you go again, making those pronouncements about what I know, what I feel. You're not inside my head, Reid."

"Sometimes it feels that way," he murmured.

Anger faded from her eyes as she lifted her hand to his cheek, whispered his name. "No matter how much you think you understand, you can't know what it's like to grapple with this. I'm walking a fine line here. One step in the wrong direction and I know I'll start screaming and never stop. I've got to get away from this, away from here."

Desperation, hard and fierce, had taken hold in his belly. "You can't leave here, Caroline. Not yet."

She bowed her head and didn't make a reply.

He couldn't let her leave. Not when she so close to being free of her past. But what could he do to keep her here?

He could say he loved her, needed her. But that love was so new to him, so unexpected, that he couldn't bring himself to say the words just yet. He needed to live with them inside him a little while longer. Even if he could tell her, would it make a difference? In Reid's life, few of the people he loved had been held or saved by the force of his tender emotions.

So he didn't appeal to her with his love. He would use another kind of love to persuade her.

Silently, he took her hand, and he pulled her out onto the front porch. "Look," he said, pointing.

She frowned. "At what?"

"At your home."

"Reid—"

"Just look, damn it."

She obeyed, and Reid knew she saw more than pastures or trees or cows ambling toward the barn for the afternoon milking. She saw what he did. A valley cupped like a lover's face between Tennessee hills. Fertile, pulsing with life, a part of her blood, its dirt ground deep in her heart. She loved this land like a person loves a mother or a father. He recognized that love, because he felt it himself.

"Can you really leave this again?" he whispered.

She said nothing.

"In spite of what happened to you here, Caroline, you love this land."

"That's not at issue."

"But you have to think about it. Can you run away again and not be called home?" He caught her hand once more in his, turned it palm up. "In seventeen years, were you ever really able to wash this soil off these fingers?"

Caroline snatched her hand away, balling it into a fist at her side, thinking that her ex-husband had once said she'd always be a farm girl. "I don't understand how I can love this place so much. I was so unhappy here. So afraid. I'm afraid now, and yet . . ." The words drifted away, much as her gaze drifted once more to the ridge that rose green against the cloudless blue sky.

She didn't know why Reid should be able to see into her heart so well. But he knew that leaving this valley again would be like tearing out a part of herself.

While she was growing up here, the big house on the hill had been filled with shadows—her grandfather's disdain, her mother's slide into insanity. But in this valley she had also seen the sunshine of life—in the scamper of a calf, in the scent of honeysuckles in the spring, in the knowledge that those who shared her blood had walked these paths before her. She had once escaped into cool autumn mornings on the ridge, summer afternoons at the creek with Lainey, frosty winter nights under star-swept skies with Kevin. And since returning, she had once again picked up the simple rhythms of the land.

If only those rhythms could heal her, shield her forever from the shadows. How sad to know that couldn't be.

Reid slipped an arm around her shoulder and whispered low against her ear, "This is your home, Caroline."

"Home shouldn't be filled with fear."

"Did the fear leave when you ran away before?"

"It faded—"

"But it came back. And you came here. Because you know this is where you belong."

Dear God, she wanted to believe him. For in leaving this valley, she knew she would lose him. It was unthinkable that he would leave. Like her Uncle Coy, like Lainey, he would wither and die anywhere else.

And so might she. Losing him would do her in. But if she stayed, with him—

"You have to stay here," he said, breaking into her thoughts. "And you have to remember."

That last assertion snapped her gaze up to his. It came back to this. To the impossible. For half a minute she had allowed herself to be seduced by sweet thoughts of living here with him. What a mistake.

Reid began, "When you remember—"

"I can't," she said flatly.

To his credit, he didn't disagree this time. He didn't push her. He didn't try wheedling her with all the arguments he had employed before. He just stood where he was, and his arm tightened around her and his cheek pressed against her hair.

But even as he brought her close, Reid could feel the distance that was opening between them. Her past and her pain were reaching out to pull them apart. And only Caroline had the power to stop it.

"Do you remember being sixteen?"

That question from Lainey made Caroline look up from the candles she was pushing into Sammi's birthday cake. "Why do you ask?"

Lainey nodded toward the window over the sink in Reid's kitchen. "I was just looking out at the party and all those jumping hormones and trying to remember being that age."

"Now, now," Caroline said. "We're not supposed to be spying on Sammi and her friends. That was the deal she struck with her father after he said there was no way the party was going to be unchaperoned like she wanted."

"So what's he doing?" Lainey murmured, jerking her head toward Reid, who was standing near the back door, sipping coffee and surveying the backyard where Sammi's sweet sixteen party was in full swing.

Caroline sighed. "He's being an overprotective father."

"He does overprotective really well," Lainey whispered back, grinning. But the smile died quickly. "Did you get a chance to talk to him like Sammi wanted?"

With another sigh, Caroline said, "I just didn't find the right moment to bring up the subject of Kirk Williams."

Since yesterday's confrontation, she and Reid had been tiptoeing around each other. He didn't seem angry. Just distant. She had feared she'd do more harm than good by bringing up Kirk. And yet Sammi, with her chin jutting at a stubborn angle, had told Caroline that Kirk was coming anyway. She had ignored Caroline's advice to the contrary. And instead of borrowing trouble and telling Reid, Caroline had chosen to believe his daughter was just blowing off steam.

So far so good. The driveway was crowded with automobiles, a testimony to Sammi's popularity, but none of them belonged to Kirk. Under the Japanese lanterns Caroline and Sammi had bought and strung in the backyard, several dozen teenagers were clustered in groups or dancing to the loud music that blared from a CD player. They had consumed mass quantities of the soft drinks, chips and dips that had been placed on the tables beneath the trees in the backyard. If anything alcoholic was being sneaked into the drinks or anything narcotic was being smoked or used, it was very well hidden. Caroline, though not a fool, hoped nothing would spoil the small-town innocence of this party. So far, it looked like the far-off thunder and a slight chance of rain might be the only trouble.

Lainey, who had been told about Kirk, asked, "What do you think will happen if he has the nerve to show up?"

"Maybe Reid won't notice. There are a lot of kids out there."

Lainey rolled her eyes. "Dream on, cousin. That man over there doesn't miss much."

No, he didn't, Caroline agreed silently. Reid Mc-Clure was a sharp, perceptive and maddeningly persistent man. He was also passionate. And caring. And she loved him so very much.

The hollowness she had been fighting bloomed in her chest, threatening to overtake her. She was torn, wanting so desperately to be with Reid, yet so afraid to stay. She had been nervous and jumpy ever since yesterday, unable to concentrate on more than the simplest task. And she had slept only in fits and bursts last night. It was as if her mind wouldn't allow her to think too hard or drop too deeply into a nightmare-ridden sleep.

"Oh, no."

Lainey's murmured exclamation drew Caroline's attention back to the window. A new car had come up the driveway and was pulling into a spot near the edge of the yard. The lights on the outside of the nearest barn and the house highlighted the car's low-slung sporty lines.

"Is that Kirk's?" Caroline whispered to Lainey, whose look said it all.

Caroline darted a glance across the room at Reid, who was still peering out the door. Maybe she could create a distraction. "You know you're violating the terms of a contract," she told him.

He gave a sheepish grin. "I can't see much from here. The screened porch is in the way."

"Then why don't you give it up?" Lainey told him, quickly following Caroline's lead. "Let me freshen that coffee."

"We could go in the living room," Caroline suggested. "We'll see if we can catch the last of that baseball game you wanted to watch."

Reid laughed. "You? Watch baseball?"

"I could become a fan."

Shaking his head, Reid looked out the window again. "I think I'll stay right here. At least until Sammi notices—" He stopped, straightening as he peered forward.

Beside Caroline, Lainey muttered a short but descriptively apt curse. Because something had hit the fan.

Reid stalked out of the house, with the two women hot on his heels.

At the edge of the crowd, Sammi waited, her arm threaded through Kirk's. She looked defiant, as if she had expected this scene.

To Reid's credit, he didn't raise his voice. He simply walked up to them and said, "Kirk, you're not welcome here."

"It's my party," Sammi shot back.

"And I don't want to ruin it," Reid said. "I'm sure you don't want to ruin it, either, Kirk. So why don't you get in your fancy car and get out of here."

Caroline saw the muscles that worked in the young man's throat. He met Reid's gaze head-on, then he looked at Sammi. "Maybe this wasn't too smart."

"So you have some brains, after all," Reid muttered.

It was an unnecessarily smart remark, and Caroline didn't really blame Kirk for taking a threatening step forward. But she wasn't going to stand here and let this get out of control.

"Reid," she said, taking hold of his arm. "Keep your cool." So far, only a few of the other teenagers seemed to have noticed what was going on. She wanted to keep it that way.

"Oh, don't bother, Caroline," Sammi said, tossing her long curls as she looked at her father. "I honestly thought he wouldn't do this, that maybe tonight of all nights, he'd cut me a little slack."

"Not with this boy," Reid said tightly. "You're not going to see him tonight or ever."

But Sammi was intent on pushing him to the limit. "You just try and stop me."

Caroline quickly stepped between Reid and his daughter. "Sammi, stop it. You're just making this worse. Why would you want to spoil your party like this?"

"I told you Kirk was coming," Sammi retorted.

"What?" Reid demanded. "You told her?"

"I didn't believe her," Caroline said, turning to face him.

"Well, believe this," Sammi snapped. "Now I'm leaving with Kirk. And nobody's going to stop me!"

She took Kirk's hand and took a step toward his car while Reid lunged around Caroline.

Only Kirk didn't move. He stood his ground and brought them all to a stop with, "Just hold it, Sammi, I'm not taking you anywhere."

Chapter Ten

Caroline raked a bowl of leftover chips into the trash with a sarcastic, "Well, what a lovely party."

"It could have been worse," Lainey said from beside the kitchen table. "Sammi could have left with Kirk."

"That's right," Caroline returned. "Now all we have is Sammi upstairs, locked in her room, crying because this boy she's crazy about walked away from her rather than fight with her father. Her friends are all gone. And Reid is out in the yard, tearing down Japanese lanterns like there's no tomorrow. What a happy, happy birthday."

As if to punctuate her remarks, Reid threw open the back door, his expression thunderous.

Lainey glanced at him and set aside the candles she had pulled out of the uneaten cake. "I'm going home," she announced.

"Thanks for your help," Reid said tightly.

"Anytime." The redhead looked at Caroline, hesitated, then merely murmured good-night before leaving.

The silence that followed was heavy with tension.

"Go ahead and say it," Caroline challenged Reid. She was tired and irritated enough to want to have it out with him. "I should have told you about Kirk."

"That's fairly obvious."

"Like that would have stopped anything. Sammi was spoiling for a fight. She would have done something like this no matter if you knew or not."

Reid opened the refrigerator door and shoved several six-packs of unopened soft drinks inside. "At least Kirk showed some sense."

"I'd show some sense, too, if an angry two-hundred-pound father was bearing down on me."

"Maybe we've seen the last of him."

Caroline snorted. "You can be such an obtuse jerk."

Reid wheeled around. "What did you say?"

"You heard me." She tossed the empty plastic bowl onto the table with more than necessary force.

"Care to explain?"

"If it's not this boy, it'll be another. If it's not a boy, it'll be something else. You've got to let up on Sammi."

"She's *my* daughter, remember."

"And you have no objectivity about anything she does. If she steps outside the parameters you've set up, you lose it." Caroline threw up her hands in disgust.

"Honest to God, Reid, I thought you were changing a little bit. Maybe Sammi thought so, too. But we were both wrong."

He glared at her. "I have a responsibility to set up those parameters."

"Why don't you just hobble her out in the yard? That'd rein her in."

His lips thinned. "I think maybe you ought to stay out of this."

"Oh, good, good," Caroline said with a sneer. "Just close it down in that special way you have, Reid. Set your jaw and say it's your way or no way. That's so effective. It's always worked so well. I know Kevin appreciated your flexibility."

Crimson spread over Reid's cheeks at the mention of his brother. "Leave him out of this," he muttered.

But Caroline was ripe for a confrontation. "You mean tap-dance around the subject of Kevin like we've done ever since we started sleeping together? No way, Reid."

Reid took a step toward her, obviously battling for control. "Just drop it."

"No. It's time to talk about Kevin. Maybe if you do, you'll realize that you're making the same mistakes with Sammi that you made with him."

"Mistakes?" he repeated. "Oh, so now you know better than me how to handle my responsibilities."

"I know your tight-fisted, closed-mind approach doesn't work."

"Well, then, what do you advocate? What would you tell Sammi? Or would you just encourage her to run away? That's your standard approach. You run from problems, from any situation you don't like.''

That stung, and while she was gathering herself for a comeback, Reid struck again. ''If *you* hadn't run away, Kevin wouldn't have gone after you. He'd be alive. So don't be preaching to me about *my* mistakes.''

She managed a short, mirthless laugh. ''I have no idea why you keep clinging to this twisted bit of logic about Kevin's death being my fault. Unless, of course, you're trying not to blame yourself.''

The stricken look that came and then was quickly banked in his eyes told Caroline she had hit a nerve. She didn't really want to hurt Reid, but she also wanted the issue of Kevin cleared away between them for good. ''That's it, isn't it? You know your own responsibility for his leaving, but admitting that is more than you can stand. The guilt's too much.''

''Talk about twisted logic,'' he said, but as he turned away, she again saw the truth in his expression.

She set aside her anger but not her determination as she stepped in front of him, effectively boxing him into a corner of the kitchen. ''Before I ever left, you were driving Kevin away, Reid. You kept trying to make his decisions for him. You wouldn't listen to his ideas or his concerns.''

''You don't know what went on between me and my brother.''

''But he told me. He told me everything.''

Reid's mouth twisted bitterly. ''And you gave him such good advice, didn't you? That's why he's dead.''

"He's dead because he was in a terrible accident. Neither you nor I had anything to do with that."

"Yes . . . you . . . did," Reid ground out. "You left . . . and he . . . he . . ."

His struggle to cling to his blame of her and deny his own feelings of guilt was painful to watch. Caroline reached out, gripping his hands in her own. "Kevin left here because he wanted to, Reid, because it was time for him to go, time for him to spread his wings. Now maybe you forced the issue some, made him want to go, but you certainly didn't cause his death."

"Of course I didn't," Reid denied a little too vehemently.

Yet he couldn't stop thinking of the dream that had come to him earlier this summer. The dream of Kevin's return and the way his brother turned to dust in Reid's hands. That dream was Caroline's fault. From the moment she had come back here, she had been trying to make him take responsibility for Kevin's leaving. Little by little, she had poked holes in his blame of her. But to actually admit it to himself, to take that blame, to accept that guilt, was so hard, too hard.

"You have to face it," she said now, her face pale and earnest as she looked up at him. "After all these years, you've got to face how you feel about this."

But because confronting his own demons was more than Reid could take tonight, he hit back at her with the anger he always summoned when hurt. "You're a fine one to talk about facing anything, Caroline."

"We're not discussing me—"

"But why shouldn't we? While you're telling me to face my feelings, why don't you face your own. Why don't you face your fears?"

She dropped his hands, her features hardening again. "You just can't stop, can you? You have to keep hammering and hammering at a person. You've just got to prove that you're right." She spun away on one heel. "I can see why Kevin wanted to get away from you."

"The same as you do."

She pivoted to face him again. "What?"

"You're leaving, aren't you? It's easier to leave than to *face* what you came here to face. You're running away again."

"I'm running because I have to."

"You're a coward."

Her face crumpled. And there were no more sharp retorts. She just left.

Reid didn't follow. He was through running after her. Through trying to help her. Through with her completely, he told himself. From the start he had known she would bring him nothing but trouble. And now...

Now she had made him love her.

Now she had made him face the truth about Kevin.

Outside, Caroline's car roared to life. Reid closed his eyes, listening to the engine fade in the distance while he tried to fight what he knew to be true. He paced around the kitchen and, feeling caged, went outside onto the screened porch. Thunder was rumbling over the valley. Rain hung heavy in the humid air. He sat down, heavy with sorrow.

And finally, sitting there, he gave in to the feelings he had masked for so many years by blaming Caroline for Kevin's loss. The sham was ripped aside. He admitted his own part in what had happened to his brother. He accepted the responsibility for Kevin's departure and death, just as he had accepted responsibility for this farm and his brother when he was eighteen years old. It was his fault. All his fault.

Kevin's dust was on his hands.

Reid had no idea how long he sat on the dimly lit porch, listening to the thunder and staring down at his hands. It could have been hours. It could have been only a few minutes.

But gradually, as he faced his feelings, he began to see the real truth. The truth Caroline had spoken. That Kevin had been ready to leave. That Reid had made errors in the way he'd dealt with his brother. But that his death was a tragedy. Just an awful, aching tragedy.

Something broke apart inside of him. A weight lifted from around his heart. His hands were clean.

Lord, what a feeling. What freedom. It was the same freedom that Caroline needed. The freedom that would come if she faced her fears, if she let herself remember.

If she ran away, she would never know the truth.

If she ran away, Reid would lose her.

His heart, so light just a moment earlier, tightened again.

He was going to lose Caroline. Lose her innocent passion. Lose her touch, the sound of her laughter. Lose the thousand and ones ways in which she had filled his empty life. Lose her to a dragon.

He couldn't let it happen. Years ago his instincts had told him to help her. Instead he had taken her back to Applewood, and her life had been altered drastically. Now he had to listen to his instincts, act on them. He had to find a way to help her. But how? Should he go to her now?

He was considering that possibility when his daughter came out of the kitchen. Her eyes were red and swollen. And the defiance that had fired their confrontation earlier tonight was gone.

"I have to talk to you," she told Reid. "I want you to listen to me about Kirk." Her spirit was bowed but unbroken.

He started to dismiss her. He started to cut her off before she could begin, to tell her it was late and she should be in bed and he didn't want to hear anything about Kirk Williams anyway. Then he looked at his hands, and he thought of his brother, and he heard Caroline's voice telling him not to make the same mistakes with Sammi that he had made with Kevin.

So he sat back. "I'll listen," he said. "But I can't promise I'll agree with you. I can't even promise I won't get angry."

"Fair enough," Sammi replied. Then she began to talk.

She was a coward.

Caroline faced the truth as thunder shook the house. Cowering in the corner of the sofa with the photograph of her and Adam clutched in her hand, she listened to the dying rumbles as they spread outward like waves. Tonight even her brother's face didn't soothe her.

The thunder was getting stronger.

The storm was drawing closer.

As close as her memories.

"All right," she whispered in the sudden silence that followed the peal of thunder. "Come back, damn you. I want to remember."

Lightning flashed, but brought no new revelation. There were only the bits and pieces she had accumulated this summer. There was only the fear, the terror that was reaching out, as certain as the storm that was building from the west.

She wanted Reid. She needed the haven of his arms. She needed his love. They had parted tonight in such anger. And tomorrow she was going to leave. That anger would serve as their farewell.

Unless she went to him. Unless she swallowed her pride and went begging for his touch. His sweet and special touch. Like no other man's. The touch that helped her forget.

Tonight he would help her remember.

The clock on the mantel struck midnight. Only an hour since she had left Reid's house. An hour like an eternity. An hour with these damned and damning memories.

Flinging aside Adam's picture, she got up, grabbed her car keys and left. She had to get to Reid.

The storm unleashed its fury halfway down the drive at Applewood. Lightning lit up the big oak tree and the crumbling wall. Thunder chased Caroline down the road. Wind blew rain at the windshield.

Lightning, thunder and rain. Like another night she had known.

At Reid's house the lights were still blazing downstairs, indicating he hadn't gone to bed. Caroline parked her car at the side and scrambled through the rain to the back screened porch. From there, she could hear Reid's voice in the kitchen. His and Sammi's, raised in anger.

Caroline paused, her hand on the doorknob, wondering whether she should go in. But then the storm blew a sheet of rain across the porch and she started to open the door.

But before she did, Sammi's voice, angry and tear-filled, rose to meet her. "You still don't understand. You're not trying to understand."

And that's when the memories came. Like vines sprouting out of the floor, they took hold of Caroline's limbs, dragged her back to the past....

She stood on the kitchen porch at Applewood. Rain was streaming down the gutters, thunder roaring overhead. She was cowering, her grandfather loomed over her. Tall and furious, screaming at her about Kevin. It seemed like forever that he had been standing over her, screaming this way.

"You can't be like your mother," Robert Parrish roared. "You can't lay down with just anyone. Your mother did. She ruined her life, ruined our name. You're not much, but you're all I've got, and I won't let you ruin yourself. Not over that McClure boy."

Caroline pressed back against the wall. "Grandfather, I haven't done anything. Kevin's just a friend. You don't understand. I've been trying to tell you, but you still don't understand.''

"Don't lie, Caroline. Don't you ever, ever lie to me.''

He took hold of her and, though he was old and she struggled, he shook her until she was dizzy. Shook her until the door to the kitchen slammed open.

Caroline's mother swayed in the doorway. "What in the hell are you two doing? You could wake the dead.''

"Or the drunk?'' Grandfather sneered.

The amber liquid in the glass she held sloshed over the rim as she swayed on her feet. "I'm not drunk.''

"You're always drunk. You're drunk and you're slovenly and you're no good to me anymore. You couldn't catch a decent husband if your life depended on it.''

With a motion that was a travesty of flirtation, Caroline's mother pushed a hand through hair that had once been a thick and glossy brown but now lay like straw against her skull. "I catch plenty of men.''

Horrified, Caroline pleaded, "Stop it, Mother. Please just stop it.''

But her mother ignored her. She was intent on Grandfather. "Any old man will do,'' she said. "Just as long as he's the opposite of one you would choose for me.''

With a roar of fury, Grandfather slapped her across the face.

Mother just laughed at him, while a horrified Caroline, who had never seen her grandfather this angry, begged them both to stop.

"Shut up," Grandfather told Caroline. "Shut up and get up to your room. You're not going to sneak off with that McClure boy again. I've got plans for you."

That snapped her mother's laughter. "What do you mean?" she demanded. "What plans?"

"You won't find a decent husband. Maybe she will."

"No." Mother reached out and hauled Caroline across the doorstep and behind her. "Just because they're gonna take the mill away, that's no reason for you to bother her. You leave her alone."

"What do you care about her?" Grandfather demanded. "I could have gotten rid of her at the same time as I got rid of the boy and you'd never have noticed."

"What do you mean?"

"The boy, remember? Your son?"

Adam, Caroline thought. What about Adam?

"I got rid of him and that Indian of yours."

"John left," Mother whispered. "He left and took Adam."

"Like I told him to."

Mother was swaying again. The ice was rattling in her glass. "They're dead," she mumbled hoarsely. "Both of them dead."

Grandfather's laugh was as loud as the thunder that was rumbling outside. He shoved his face close to Mother's and said, "You think they're dead? Think again."

The glass fell from Mother's hand and smashed on the floor. She slipped on the bourbon and the slivers of glass and ice as she lunged for Grandfather's face.

He caught her and laughed even harder, while Caroline covered her ears with her hands. Adam, she thought, my Adam. He's not dead.

The words that had fueled Grandfather's laughter gave Mother strength. She was hitting him, screaming for her husband and son. Finally, Caroline leapt forward and pulled her off. Grandfather escaped the kitchen and made for the front hall.

When he was gone, Mother was suddenly, frighteningly still. She turned and took Caroline by the shoulders. "We're leaving here."

"Mother, please—"

"We're leaving right now. We're getting away from him."

There was a clearness in her gaze that Caroline hadn't seen in years. A clearness and a hope. A bright, shining hope.

"We're going to find your father and your brother," Mother whispered. "I think I know where to look. I think I know where they are."

She was drunk, but Caroline wanted to believe her. Wanted it more than she had ever wanted anything in her life. So she took her hand and they went out in the rain, and Mother climbed behind the wheel of her big, old car. Caroline wanted to drive, knew she should drive, but Mother insisted that she could do it. She rolled down the window and turned her face up to the rain and laughed. A young laugh. A free laugh.

"We're going to find Adam," she told Caroline.

They took off, but the car stalled just past the front of the house.

That's when Grandfather came running outside.

He was screaming. Mother screamed, too, and pumped on the gas pedal. The car shuddered to life just as Grandfather reached them. It shot forward in the rain, while Grandfather ran beside it. Running, reaching, bellowing like a dragon.

"Get away," Mother screamed back at him, even as she fought off his hands, which tried to grab the steering wheel. *"Get away.* You stole my boy! You stole my Adam!"

With that, she floored the gas pedal. Grandfather was left behind. They spun off into the thunder and the lightning and the rain.

They were free.

Free, except for the tree at the end of the drive. It rose to meet them, and Caroline screamed . . .

The door separating the back porch from the kitchen was wrenched open, out of her hands, and Caroline looked up into Reid's face. Sammi crowded close behind him, both of them demanding to know what was wrong and why she had screamed.

Realizing why, she fell back a step. She blinked and saw her mother, her grandfather, felt the crash of the car.

"Caroline, what's wrong?" Reid said, reaching for her hand.

But she snatched it back. And then she ran. Through the rain, with Reid and Sammi calling her name, splashing after her. She made it to her car, slammed the door and started the engine just as Reid grabbed the door handle and pulled it open.

Was it Reid?

Or was it the dragon?

With that question thundering as loud as the storm, she scrambled across the seat and out the other side of the car. She ran through the rain, toward the main road. She could hear someone calling her name, but she didn't stop. Didn't stop until she slipped in the mud and fell onto the cold, wet ground.

Her face scraped across gravel. She tasted blood in her mouth. The rain beat into her. Thunder made the world spin in front of her. But when she looked up, she saw him. In the lightning that split the sky, she saw the dragon. He had her mother.

He was pounding her head into the ground.

Gripped by blind, senseless fury, he pounded the life out of her mother.

And then he looked up, looked right at Caroline. He knew she had seen him. And now she was next. He was coming for her.

Great heaving sobs tore through Caroline as the memory came back. She could see the blue lights that had cut through the night. Sheriff Leavitt had found her, soothed her. She had tried hard, so hard, to tell him what her grandfather had done, but she couldn't force the words out. She kept seeing the dragon's eyes, glittering through the rain, daring her to tell. She was so afraid, so desperately afraid, that it was better not to tell. It was better to forget.

Only that was wrong, Caroline realized now as she rolled onto her back and let the rain hit her face. It wasn't better to forget. It was best to remember. Because these memories, however horrible, were like the rain. They were washing her clean.

From out of the rain, Reid pounded to her side, slid down on his knees, calling her name.

She sat up and went into his embrace.

"God in heaven, Caroline," he murmured, gripping her tight to him. "What's wrong?"

"I remember," she told him, holding tight to her anchor in any storm. She couldn't stop repeating those sweet, sweet words. "I remember."

Chapter Eleven

There had been many cloudless, perfect days in the past year. But none more beautiful than this, Caroline thought. The August sun was warm on her face. The front yard at Applewood was filled with friends and family. At her side was the man she loved. In her arms was their son.

Christopher Kevin McClure. Two months old today. Christened this morning with half the population of Parrish County looking on.

He'd had a big day, what with church and this christening party that Lainey had insisted on throwing. He'd been passed from one admiring person to the next and had barely complained. But now he'd had enough, and he expressed his displeasure quite vocally.

"Come on, big fella," Reid admonished, taking him from Caroline. "Don't be that way." The baby's cry faded to a whimper at his father's touch.

"He looks just like you when he's complaining," Caroline said, leaning back in her chair. "He gets all red and screws up his mouth."

"That's not very complimentary." With expert ease, Reid lifted his fussing son to his shoulder.

Sammi came up the big house's front steps to the chairs where Reid and Caroline sat alone. A very grown-up Sammi, sporting a sleek, short, new haircut, but with the same saucy style as ever. "Dad, Chris doesn't like being held like that. Give him to me."

"He likes it the same as you liked it when you were his age," Reid shot back. "Go on, now, and leave your brother alone. Doesn't Kirk need you or something?"

With a roll of her eyes, Sammi went back down the steps to rejoin Kirk and a group of their friends. The young man looped an arm casually over her shoulders, and Reid grumbled something deep in his throat.

"Oh, please," Caroline admonished him. "They've been going out ever since you relented last fall. It's about time you gave up the overprotective father routine."

"I still don't trust him."

"You'll never trust anyone with her."

"I'm just glad Christopher is a boy."

She harrumphed. "You'll find something to worry about with him, too."

"Probably."

"And if we ever have another baby..."

"If?" Reid murmured. "After this morning, it might be when."

Caroline's gaze met his and clung, a flush stealing into her face as she recalled how he had come to her in the shower this morning while the rest of the household was sleeping. How he had pressed her against the wall. How he had stroked her. Filled her. Caught her cries of completion beneath his mouth. Remembering, she felt perspiration pool in the valley between her breasts and heat quicken in the delta at the juncture of her thighs. He could make her hot with just a glance. That hadn't changed in nearly one year of marriage. She doubted it would ever change.

"Stop looking at me that way," she told him, glancing out at the guests in the yard. "Everybody'll see what you're thinking."

He grinned cockily. "I don't mind everybody knowing that I can make my wife squirm in her chair." He leaned closer, his voice lowering seductively. "How about if we give Christopher to Sammi and sneak inside. There's sure to be an empty room. What I'd like…" His voice dipped even lower, strummed across her nerve endings as he outlined in graphic detail exactly what he would like to do to her.

Instead of admonishing him, Caroline widened her eyes and asked, "Do you really think we could do that?"

"I can do anything," Reid murmured as he leaned forward to kiss her.

"I love you," she whispered as he drew away. "I love you so much, Reid. I couldn't be any happier."

"Me, too." Reid drank in the beauty of her glowing features. This year with this remarkable woman had taught him what real love could be. He now understood that the power of love could heal you, save you. He possessed that power with Caroline. For a man who had tried to shoulder the responsibilities of the world for most of his life, it was awesome to realize how much lighter the load was with this slim, strong woman at his side.

He smiled at her, something he tried to do at least a hundred times a day. "Have I told you lately how much I love you?"

"I'm always willing to hear an update."

Just as Reid was about to comply, their son set up another protest.

Sighing, Caroline pulled away and stood. "I think it's time for this little boy to be fed. I'm going to go inside and see if I can get him to sleep, as well."

She took Christopher and went inside. Without a qualm, she went into the house that had once fed her fears. She had beaten the dragon.

Reid stood, surveying the view from the porch at Applewood. Lainey's flowers were in full bloom. The grass was green. The orchard fanned out in long, lush rows of trees. The scene was peaceful, serene, a calm facade that had once hidden so much pain.

Robert Parrish had murdered his daughter at the end of the long, curving drive. Beneath the oak tree that had stood sentinel over his family's home for generations. Caroline had seen it happen. Robert knew she had seen him. And thus, because she feared what he might do to her, as well, her mind had allowed her to forget.

After Caroline had remembered, Reid had wanted her to go to the authorities. But she had refused. Proving anything now would be a difficult process. Reid was unsure. He was suspicious of the coroner's report, wondered if Robert Parrish might have paid someone off.

Caroline had pointed out that the report said her mother died of massive head injuries. Because it was clear that Linda Parrish had hit the windshield, it might never have been easy to determine what blow had killed her. Caroline was certain that her mother was alive after the accident. She had seen her struggling against Robert. Caroline knew he had killed her. But as for making that public knowledge, she preferred not to.

She had made peace with the past. Reid admired her for that. It would have been understandable that she might continue to be haunted by that night, by the nightmarish image of her grandfather taking her mother's life. And if not that, there were the days that had followed the accident. Days in which a nameless, faceless fear had first wrapped around Caroline's soul. Now she understood where that fear had come from. She understood why her grandfather had watched her with such fierce intensity right after the accident, why he wouldn't let her talk about it, why he tried to purge the house of any reminder of her mother.

Caroline wanted to believe her grandfather had been torn by guilt for what he had done. She had talked to Sheriff Leavitt again, had finally taken comfort from the man's description of the anguished way Robert

Parrish had rocked Linda's body in his arms, wailing her name and crying in the rain.

Reid wasn't so forgiving. Even now, anger clenched his gut when he considered what might have happened if Sheriff Leavitt hadn't come along when he had. Would Robert Parrish have silenced Caroline the same way he'd killed his daughter? Reid wasn't sure.

It was a question Caroline had stopped considering. What she did consider, frequently, was what might have happened to her twin brother.

Reid frowned. Adam was the only cloud in their otherwise perfect world. Now that she knew he might be alive, Caroline yearned to find her brother.

A few months after their wedding last September, she had begun a search on her own, but had soon met a brick wall. Lainey was the one who had hired a private investigator, using the money that Coy had set aside from the farm's profits, the money Caroline hadn't wanted. Men named Adam Cutler had been located from Maine to California. None of them had panned out. Not yet, anyway.

The door behind Reid opened, and he turned to greet his wife and Lainey, as well. They moved out into the crowd of friends and neighbors, saying goodbye as the afternoon began to fade.

It was on the lawn, after the last guests had departed, that Lainey bent to pick up a discarded napkin and a photograph slipped out of the pocket of her full, navy cotton skirt.

"What's this?" Caroline asked, retrieving it. The answer was obvious as she studied the picture.

It was the snapshot Lainey had found in the attic last year. The one of Caroline and Adam with their parents.

Filled with a familiar sadness, Caroline touched their faces. "I'd forgotten about this."

"I thought you might have," Lainey murmured. A sheepish smile curved her lips. "I was looking at it this morning, thinking that Christopher looks like Adam."

"You think so?" Caroline said, studying her brother's plump baby face.

"And he might grow up to look a little like your father." Lainey sighed, her emerald eyes, usually so steady, took on a distinctly dreamy cast. "He was so handsome."

"I wish I knew exactly why he left."

Stepping to Caroline's side, Reid said, "It was your grandfather. It had nothing to do with you."

"You know me so well, don't you?" She lifted a hand to his cheek. "You can tell what I'm thinking almost before I think it."

"That's love," Reid said. "It can be supernaturally powerful when it's right."

"The power of love," Caroline repeated, smiling at her husband.

Then she looked down at the photograph in her hand. Her father's bold Native American features sparked something inside her. Just like the first time she saw this picture, a tickle ran up the back of her neck. But not frightening this time. Just a presence. A feeling . . .

She glanced up at Reid, whose eyes had widened, as well.

They stared at one another, knowing they were feeling the same thing.

"It's eerie," Reid began.

"Wonder who that can be," Lainey said, breaking into the moment as she shaded her eyes and looked toward the road.

Caroline turned to see an old tan pickup coming up the drive. Dust-colored. Rusty. Unaccountably, it made her think of the truck her father and Adam had driven away in so many, many years ago.

It pulled to stop in front of the house. A man got out. Dark. Tall and lean. In faded jeans and a T-shirt. A cowboy hat tucked back on his head.

"Oh, my God," Lainey whispered.

That's when Caroline began to run, down the sloping yard, her arms open wide, calling her brother's name.

The picture she had held was dropped. It blew away on the breeze. Fluttering just over the truck as Caroline welcomed her brother home.

Early the next morning, Reid awoke, realized Caroline wasn't in bed, and went in search of her. He found her in the window seat in Christopher's nursery, a notepad on her knees, though she was staring out at the night.

"What's going on?" he asked.

She turned, smiling, and he slipped in behind her on the seat. "I couldn't sleep," she murmured, settling back against him.

"Too much excitement."

"I've just got everything I want now."

Her brother and the five-year-old son who had accompanied him on the drive from Canada were asleep in a room at Applewood. The private investigator had contacted him last week. And while Lainey had known there was some hope that he might have been found, she hadn't wanted to get Caroline's hopes up until all the facts had been checked out.

It seemed Adam hadn't been sure he wanted to be found. He had known where Applewood was all his life, but he had been told that Linda Parrish hadn't wanted him, that she had sent him away. His memories of Caroline had been vaguer than hers of him. Their father had died, and Adam had been adopted by a loving family. But Adam had known pain. His wife was dead. His young son was troubled.

Reid had seen a world of hurt in his eyes. He recognized that look, because he had faced it in the mirror for most of his own life. But if anyone could aid in the healing, it was Caroline.

For now, Adam and his son were staying in the valley. And Caroline was ecstatic. That's all that mattered to Reid.

"What's this?" he said, tapping the notepad on her lap.

"Notes."

"For what?"

"The last *Seers* book."

"The last?"

"It has to end," Caroline said, her eyes bright with happiness. "The prince and the princess have come home. They've won."

Reid set the notepad aside, his hands slipping around to cup her breasts through the thin cotton of her gown. "You can plot it all tomorrow. Right now, you need to employ your imagination in some other way."

She laughed, turning his arms. "You're insatiable, Mr. Reid McClure."

He dipped his mouth toward hers. "Thank goodness my wife is, too."

*   *   *   *   *

Rugged and lean...and the best-looking, sweetest-talking men to be found in the entire Lone Star state!

Diana Palmer

LONG, TALL TEXANS

In July 1994, Silhouette is very proud to bring you Diana Palmer's first three LONG, TALL TEXANS. CALHOUN, JUSTIN and TYLER—the three cowboys who started the legend. Now they're back by popular demand in one classic volume—and they're ready to lasso your heart! Beautifully repackaged for this special event, this collection is sure to be a longtime keepsake!

"Diana Palmer makes a reader want to find a Texan of her own to love!" —*Affaire de Coeur*

LONG, TALL TEXANS—the first three—reunited in this special roundup!

**Available in July,
wherever Silhouette books are sold.**

Take 4 bestselling love stories FREE

Plus get a FREE surprise gift!

Special Limited-time Offer

Mail to Silhouette Reader Service™

P.O. Box 609
Fort Erie, Ontario
L2A 5X3

YES! Please send me 4 free Silhouette Special Edition® novels and my free surprise gift. Then send me 6 brand-new novels every month, which I will receive months before they appear in bookstores. Bill me at the low price of $3.21 each plus 25¢ delivery and GST*. That's the complete price and—compared to the cover prices of $3.99 each—quite a bargain! I understand that accepting the books and gift places me under no obligation ever to buy any books. I can always return a shipment and cancel at any time. Even if I never buy another book from Silhouette, the 4 free books and the surprise gift are mine to keep forever.

335 BPA AQS3

Name	(PLEASE PRINT)	
Address	Apt. No.	
City	Province	Postal Code

This offer is limited to one order per household and not valid to present Silhouette Special Edition® subscribers. *Terms and prices are subject to change without notice.
Canadian residents will be charged applicable provincial taxes and GST.

CSPE-694   ©1990 Harlequin Enterprises Limited

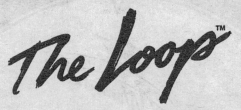

Silhouette

SPECIAL EDITION™

That
SPECIAL
Woman!

ONE OF OUR OWN
Cheryl Reavis

Getting custody of her orphaned nephew was the hardest thing Sloan Baron had ever faced. She found herself on unfamiliar New Mexico territory, forced to battle stubborn Navaho policeman Lucas Singer. Lucas was as stubborn as Sloan was feisty, but soon she found herself undeniably attracted....

Don't miss ONE OF OUR OWN, by Cheryl Reavis, available in August!

She's friend, wife, mother—she's you! And beside each Special Woman stands a wonderfully *special* man. It's a celebration of our heroines—and the men who become part of their lives.

Don't miss **THAT SPECIAL WOMAN!** each month—from some of your special authors! Only from Silhouette Special Edition!

Silhouette

SPECIAL EDITION™

WHAT EVER HAPPENED TO...?

Have you been wondering when much-loved characters will finally get their own stories? Well, have we got a lineup for you! Silhouette Special Edition is proud to present a *Spin-off Spectacular!* Be sure to catch these exciting titles from some of your favorite authors:

***HOMEWARD BOUND** (July, SE #900)* Mara Anvik is recalled to her old home for a dire mission—which reunites her with old flame Mark Toovak in *Sierra Rydell*'s exciting spin-off to ON MIDDLE GROUND (SE #772).

***BABY, COME BACK** (August, SE #903)* Erica Spindler returns with an emotional story about star-crossed lovers Hayes Bradford and Alice Dougherty, who are given a second chance for marriage in this follow-up to BABY MINE (SE #728).

***THE WEDDING KNOT** (August, SE #905)* Pamela Toth's tie-in to WALK AWAY, JOE (SE #850) features a marriage of convenience that allows Daniel Sixkiller to finally adopt...and to find his perfect mate in determined Karen Whitworth!

***A RIVER TO CROSS** (September, SE #910)* Shane Macklin and Tina Henderson shared a forbidden passion, which they can no longer deny in the latest tale from *Laurie Paige*'s WILD RIVER series.

Don't miss these wonderful titles, only for our readers— only from Silhouette Special Edition!

BABY'S CHOICE

Those mischievous matchmaking babies are back, as Marie Ferrarella's Baby's Choice series continues in August with MOTHER ON THE WING (SR #1026).

Frank Harrigan could hardly explain his sudden desire to fly to Seattle. Sure, an old friend had written to him out of the blue, but there was something else.... Then he spotted Donna McCollough, or rather, she fell right into his lap. And from that moment on, they were powerless to interfere with what angelic fate had lovingly ordained.

Continue to share in the wonder of life and love, as babies-in-waiting handpick the most perfect parents, only in

Silhouette
R O M A N C E™

BABY BLESSED
Debbie Macomber

Molly Larabee didn't expect her reunion with
estranged husband Jordan to be quite so explosive.
Their tumultuous past was filled with memories of
tragedy—and love. Rekindling familiar passions left
Molly with an unexpected blessing...and suddenly a
future with Jordan was again worth fighting for!

Don't miss Debbie Macomber's fiftieth book,
BABY BLESSED, available in July!

She's friend, wife, mother—she's you! And beside
each **Special Woman** stands a wonderfully
special man. It's a celebration of our heroines—
and the men who become part of their lives.

by Christine Rimmer

Three rapscallion brothers. Their main talent: making trouble. Their only hope: three uncommon women who knew the way to heal a wounded heart! Meet them in these books:

Jared Jones

hadn't had it easy with women. Retreating to his mountain cabin, he found willful Eden Parker waiting to show him a good woman's love in MAN OF THE MOUNTAIN (May, SE #886).

Patrick Jones

was determined to show Regina Black that a wild Jones boy was *not* husband material. But that wouldn't stop her from trying to nab him in SWEETBRIAR SUMMIT (July, SE #896)

Jack Roper

came to town looking for the wayward and beautiful Olivia Larrabee. He never suspected he'd uncover a long-buried Jones family secret in A HOME FOR THE HUNTER (September, SE #908)....

Meet these rascal men and the women who'll tame them, only from Silhouette Books and Special Edition!